ZERO G

For Melissa —

ZERO G

THE ZERO CHRONICLES: BOOK 1

DAN WELLS

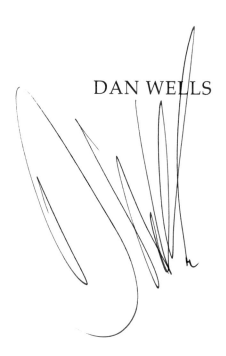

Prince
of
Cats
Literary
Productions

CONTENTS

DEDICATION

*This book is dedicated
to the real life Zero:
my son Noah*

CHAPTER 1
ABASSI STATION

IT'S HARD TO CHOOSE A FAVORITE THING ABOUT OUTER SPACE, but if Zero Huang had to pick just one, it would be gravity. Or more specifically, the complete *lack* of gravity. Planets were pretty cool, but in space he could fly.

Which was why, waiting in the giant line to board the Pathfinder, he was sitting on the ceiling.

"You're supposed to hold the railing," said his mother. She, of course, was holding the railing tightly. Zero's mom *always* followed the rules. In fact, looking up and down the long, straight hallway on Abassi Station, almost all of the passengers were holding on to the railing, grasping it tightly to keep from floating away. The only ones who weren't were kids like Zero, though at twelve years old, he was probably the oldest of the goof-offs. All of them were wearing the one-piece coverall that marked them as Pathfinder passengers.

"Just hold the stupid railing, Zero," said Yen. He was Zero's middle brother, almost fifteen years old, and always acted like he was in charge.

"Don't call him Zero," said their father, his nose deep in

a book—not a tablet book like a normal person reads, but a real, old, dead-tree book like they used to read in the olden days. He wasn't holding the railing either—instead he had his foot hooked under a bar that ran along the floor. That's how the real space travelers did it, he'd told them. Keep your foot under the bar and you can stay in one place and use both your hands, just like on Earth. Zero's father was kind of an expert in that stuff—after all, he was one of the engineers who'd built the Pathfinder. Yaozu Huang had spent most of the last five years on Abassi Station, overseeing the construction. Zero still thought he was probably wrong about the floor bars, though, because why would a real space traveler want to stick to the floor like that? *You could literally fly up here.* Railings were for losers.

Zero's parents hated it when his brothers called him Zero, but Zero didn't mind it. Anything was better than his real name, Su-Shu, because then his brothers would call him—

"You mean Two-Shoe," said Park.

Yep, that's what they'd call him. It wasn't even an insult. Zero didn't know why they called him that, but he still hated it, which, he supposed, was probably why they called him that.

"Come on down, Two-Shoe," said Yen with a laugh.

"Put those Two-Shoes on the floor!" Park laughed with him.

"My name is Zero!"

Park was Zero's oldest brother, already sixteen, which was apparently old enough that he considered his brothers to be completely beneath his notice. Most of the time, at least. If he was teasing Zero now, that probably meant he was bored.

Better bored than cranky, Zero decided. Park had a girl-friend, but her family wasn't part of the Pathfinder mission. He could text her for a few more hours—Abassi Station had great reception—but then they'd board the ship, settle in, take off, and Park would never see her again.

They'd never see anyone again, really, unless that person were on the Pathfinder, too. Or maybe the Torchbearer. After more than a century of searching, the human race had finally found two habitable planets, called Genji and Kaguya, orbiting a star called Murasaki, and they'd built two colony ships to go out and settle them. The Torchbearer mission had left last month, and last week it had cleared the solar system and Boosted the Medina StarDrive, accelerating to almost one-fifth of light speed. In about a month, Pathfinder would clear the solar system and do the same. But even at that speed, the journey would take a very long time. Murasaki was more than twenty light-years away.

The Pathfinder, and everyone on it, would be traveling for 105 years.

Everyone in line moved about four paces forward and then stopped. Another family had boarded. Zero pushed off from the ceiling, floated forward to catch up with his family, and then reached out a hand to push off of Yen's head, settling himself back up against the ceiling. Yen slapped at him with his free hand, but it was too late, and Zero laughed, just out of reach. Yen sneered, let go of the railing, and kicked off from the floor to attack him. He got high enough to poke Zero in the ear before their mother caught him by the leg and pulled him back down.

"Hold on to the railing," she said.

Yen looked offended. "Zero's not!"

"He's not starting fights, either," said their mother.

"He pushed my head!" shouted Yen.

"Stop shouting," said their father, calmly turning a page in his book.

Yen scowled, but hooked his foot under the floor bar and crossed his arms in a huff. Zero rubbed his ear where Yen had poked him, and tried to decide the best way to get revenge. He thought for a minute, and got an idea so horrible it made him smile.

He started quietly spitting, forming a blob of saliva in the air in front of him; it floated in the hallway like a water balloon without the balloon—a full sphere of solid spit. It took him a few minutes to get it nice and big, and the line advanced a few more times; he tapped the bubble, trying to make it move, but all that did was break off a few smaller droplets. Zero caught them before they floated onto any of the other people in line, and guided them back to the larger bubble. He played with it for a bit and found that if he pushed on the air with his palms, the little air currents would move the water.

He gathered all the spit back into one big spitball, pushed it toward his family, and gave it a double-handed air shove straight at Yen's head. That didn't work nearly as well as he'd hoped: instead of flying toward Yen the spitball simply rippled and stayed in place, and then Zero's hands slammed into it, and the ball splashed into dozens of tiny spit drops that flew in every direction at once.

Zero shouted a warning, but only some of the people got out of the way: spit flew into his mother's hair, and into the hair and clothes and faces of the people standing near them in line. One drop even hit a page of his dad's book. It seemed like everyone got spit on them *except* Yen, but that didn't stop Yen from kicking off of the floor again and flying up to tackle Zero against the ceiling. Their spit-covered neighbors gasped and shrieked, and their mom snapped at them, and their dad roared at them to come down. Park yanked them both down, and their parents said "Stop it this instant!" in one of those really angry whispers parents use when they're in public. They put Yen at the back of the family, and Zero at the front, and Zero hooked his foot under the lower railing and waited.

An hour later, they reached the front of the line.

CHAPTER 2

THE BOARDING AGENT

WHEN THEY FINALLY REACHED THE FRONT, THEY SAW THAT THE line was splitting into five different minilines, each one leading to a small desk and a door. Zero's heart sped up, and he got excited—this was it! Those doors led into the Pathfinder starship! He was in the front of his family, so he walked right past the desk and tried to go through the doorway. The woman at the desk stopped him with a cheerful smile.

"Whoa, there! Not quite ready for that yet." She looked at Zero's mom. "Last name?"

"Huang," said his mom, and spelled it for her: "H-U-A-N-G."

"Excellent," said the woman at the desk, and typed the name into the computer. "Are you ... Yaozu and Yubi?"

"That's us," said his father.

She looked at the three boys. "And you three must be Park, Wenyan, and Su-Shu."

Yen raised his finger. "That's spelled T-W-O-S-H-O-E—"

"Stop it," said their mother, but she smiled as she said it, trying to look like a normal, happy family. She handed the boarding agent a stack of slim plastic cards. "That's us, all right. Here are our IDs."

"Thank you." The woman at the desk scanned each card across her screen, one at a time. "Oh! Mr. Huang, it says here you were one of our engineers for the Pathfinder! Thank you so much for your work! It's a beautiful ship."

"Thank you," said Zero's father.

"Your stasis pods are in Section C, Ring 181," said the woman. "That's right next to one of the main exits, so you'll be some of the very first people to get off the ship when you arrive at Kaguya Colony tomorrow!"

"Golden," said Park.

"Wait," said Zero. "Tomorrow?"

The woman laughed—not mocking, but like Zero had just made a delightful joke. "Not tomorrow for Earth, of course, but for all of us on the ship."

"Duh," said Yen, smacking Zero in the shoulder. "We're going to be in stasis pods, remember? We're going to be asleep the whole time."

"I know that," said Zero, "but—"

"Did you really think we were going to spend a hundred years awake?" asked Yen. "Just sitting on the ship, picking our noses for a hundred—"

"Quiet," said their mother sharply, and then smiled at the desk agent. "They're very excited."

"I know about the stasis pods," said Zero, frowning. "I know it'll seem like tomorrow, but it's actually a hundred and five years."

"That's right!" said the woman brightly. "I can see *some-one's* read the intro packet." She winked at Zero, then handed the ID cards back to Zero's mom. "Thanks to engineers like your dad here, the Pathfinder is equipped with the Medina StarDrive, which will take us to the edge of the solar system in about a month. At top speed, we'll be going nearly four million kilometers per hour!"

"So you're going to be on the ship with us?" asked Park. He was using his "impress a girl" voice. Zero made a gagging face.

"I will!" said the woman. "I'm part of the Kaguya Colony administrative staff, so I'll also be one of the people processing you when it's time to leave the ship tomorrow." She smiled at Zero. "In a hundred and five years."

"Wait," said Yen. "The Medina drive is way faster than four million kilometers an hour. Isn't it supposed to be, like, one-fifth of light speed?"

The woman looked at their mom with a kind of gobsmacked admiration; Zero was really starting to think that this boundless cheerfulness was all just an act. "You have a family of little geniuses, don't you?" She winked at their father. "I suppose that shouldn't surprise me with an engineer like you." She looked back at Yen. "You're absolutely right: the Medina StarDrive is very fast, but once we clear the edge of the solar system, the computers will Boost it, and it will go so much faster. The Pathfinder will accelerate to one-fifth of light speed, which is almost twenty-two *trillion* kilometers per hour—that's about five point five thousand times faster than our top speed inside the solar system."

"Why can't we just hit the Boost right here?" asked Zero. He'd read *most* of the intro packet, but it had gotten really boring after the first page.

"Because one-fifth of light speed is fast enough to be

incredibly dangerous if anything gets in our way," said the woman. "Deep space is almost completely empty—we can go as fast as we want without running into anything bigger than dust, and our hull shields will be more than enough to handle those kinds of impacts. But inside the solar system we have planets, we have moons, we have asteroids—"

"There's an asteroid belt," said Park, obviously trying to impress her.

"There are *two* asteroid belts," said Zero. He felt a gleeful victory when the woman smiled at him instead of at Park.

"That's right!" she said. She tapped on the screen, and a new set of plastic cards began printing through a slot in her desk. She grabbed each one as it finished, collecting them into a pile so they couldn't float away. "There's a small belt between Mars and Jupiter, and a much bigger belt beyond Neptune. That big one's called the Kuiper Belt, and it's where dwarf planets like Pluto and Eris are. It's still pretty empty compared to the smaller belt, but it's full enough that we don't risk Boosting until we get to the other side of it. Then it's clear sailing from here to Murasaki!"

"Remember when we rode on that motorboat in the lake last summer?" asked their father. "When you're still in the harbor you have to go super slow—they call it 'wakeless speed.' This is the same kind of thing, only ... bigger."

"Much bigger," said their mother.

"Golden," said Zero.

"These cards are the keys to your stasis pods," said the woman, handing the five new keys to Zero's mom. "They'll also be your new IDs on Kaguya Colony, so don't lose them. Now just go through this door, across the boarding bridge, and follow the signs to Section C, Ring 181. You can open your pods with those keys, get in, and then you'll wake up twenty light-years away!"

"Thank you so much," said their mother. "All right, boys, let's go."

They walked through the door and around a corner.

And then Zero saw the Pathfinder starship for the very first time.

CHAPTER 3

THE PATHFINDER

THE PATHFINDER WAS ENORMOUS. ZERO HAD ALREADY KNOWN that it was the biggest spaceship ever built—even bigger than the Torchbearer—but seeing it in person was incredible. He stopped in the hallway and stared out the window at it: a gigantic cylinder, almost a full kilometer long and more than a hundred meters wide. It was even bigger than the space station.

"It looks like a skyscraper, lying on its side," said Zero.

"It basically is," said his father, standing next to him at the window. "It would be the biggest skyscraper on Earth, too, if it was down on Earth."

Zero stared at it. "You built the whole thing in space, right?"

"We did," said his father. "That made it a lot easier, for a lot of reasons, but mostly because it meant we got to ignore gravity. It never tipped over, we never dropped anything, and when it was done we didn't have to launch it into space. All the room at the back, where we would have had to put a giant rocket booster, is just full of supplies instead."

"Zero gravity is the best," said Zero, and let go of the railing to float even higher.

"Don't get too excited," said his mother, grabbing him by the arm and pulling him back to the floor. "Let's go find our pods." She walked toward the boarding bridge, and the family followed.

"Yeah, calm down," said Yen, and flicked him in the ear as he walked past. Zero frowned and rubbed his ear, but didn't retaliate.

The boarding bridge was wider than the hallway on the station had been, and almost completely transparent, like a giant glass tube. It stretched out from Abassi Station to a door in the Pathfinder's side, and it was full of people gawking—at the ship, at the station, at space, at everything. Zero stared wide-eyed at the empty blackness around him—it was practically like floating outside in space!—and paid so little attention to where he was going that he bumped right into Park.

"Watch it, Zero." Park pushed him away, and Zero didn't have anything to grab onto, so he had to float all the way to the far wall before pushing off of it and propelling himself back toward his family. Coming back meant he was facing a different direction, which gave him a whole new distraction to look at, and he bumped into his mom this time.

"Sorry," he said quickly, and pointed out the side of the tube. "Look!"

His mother gripped Zero's arm, so he wouldn't float away again, and together they looked at the giant glowing blue marble of Earth.

"It's next to us," he said, staring in wonder. "I thought Earth was below us?"

"You're in zero gravity," said his mother. "Up and down can be whatever you want them to be."

"Cool," said Zero, and turned himself so that the Earth was under his feet. It made it look like everyone else was standing on the side of the tube instead of the bottom. "You guys look weird."

"Not as weird as you," said Park.

"Be nice," said his father. "Do you want to see inside?" They hurried through the boarding bridge toward the ship, pulling themselves along with railings, floor bars, and a series of handholds placed all over the sides of the tube. When they reached the ship they floated inside, part of a crowd of other passengers, and Zero stared in wonder. The tube carried them toward the center of the giant ship, passing a bunch of smaller aisles as they went. Each aisle was short and narrow—a perfect size for Zero, but his father and maybe even Park would have had to crouch to walk through them. The center of the ship, on the other hand, was wide-open, laced with metal struts but otherwise empty.

"This is the main route through the ship," said Zero's father. "See that?" He pointed to a group of signs, painted directly onto the metal. The first said, "Ring 90." The second showed an arrow pointing to the left and said, "Rings 1–89." The last sign pointed off to the right and said, "Rings 91–300." Zero's father floated toward the signs and tapped the one that said "Rings 1–89. "That's the back of the ship. It's called the aft," said Zero's father. "The front of the ship is called the fore. The Rings are basically like the floors of a building, so you can think of this as a skyscraper with three hundred floors."

"Our pods are in Ring 181," said Yen, taking charge and pointing toward the fore. "This way."

Their mother looked confused. "And we just ... float through the center of the ship?"

"Yep," said their father. "The outer edge of the ship is all stasis pods, and then there's an inner Ring of cargo, and then this central column is how you get around. We could go through the outer tunnels, technically, but the open center is faster." He turned himself sideways so that his head was pointing to the fore and jumped. He sailed toward the nearest metal struts, grabbed them, and turned back to look at the rest of the family. "Come on! It's fun!"

Park grinned and jumped after him. Zero turned himself the same way, ready to jump as well, but Yen pushed him hard on the arm and he flew sideways instead, bumping into a metal wall with a thud. It didn't hurt, but Zero snarled and launched himself after Yen, ready to tackle him. The trouble was, he aimed himself at where Yen started, not where Yen was going, and he couldn't change direction in midair. While the rest of the family flew gently toward the fore of the ship, Zero careened diagonally into another wall. Yen laughed again, and their mother scowled and warned them both to behave. Zero aimed himself better this time, trying to guess where Yen was headed and launch himself toward that spot, but this time he overshot, sailing far past him and all the way to the next set of metal struts. With his head pointed toward the fore of the ship, the same direction he was traveling, it felt like he was flying upward, making superhuman leaps from wall to scaffold to wall, and he laughed at the pure joy of it. He forgot all about tackling Yen, and Yen and Park forgot about teasing him, and soon the three of them were racing up the wide column, leaping and soaring like super-heroes. Zero shouted a loud "Woohoo!" as he flew, and started trying to bounce himself off the walls: aiming at one side, turning himself in midair, and then landing on his feet and kicking off again. He could go even faster than his brothers that way, and soon they were all doing it, whooping and shouting as they found new ways to play in the zero gravity. Their parents struggled to keep up, but soon they all arrived at the sign marked 'Ring 181.'

"This is it," said Yen, and looked around. "What's Section C?"

"It's those hallways we keep passing," said Park. "They're all labeled with letters. See? This one's H."

Zero looked at the tunnels branching off from the center column, found C, and launched himself toward it. He got there just ahead of Yen, and hooked his foot under one of the railings. It was about the size of a normal Earth hallway, with smaller aisles running off on either side. The aisles were marked with colors, and each one was filled—abso-lutely filled—with rows of stasis pods.

"They look like glass coffins," said Park.

Zero nodded in agreement. Most of the pods were empty, but some were already filled with sleeping people. Zero thought they looked creepy.

"Which tunnel is ours?" asked Yen.

"It's probably on those cards Mom has," said Park.

They waited, staring at the sleeping faces inside the stasis pods, until their parents caught up.

Their father pointed toward the far end of the hallway. "See that bulkhead?" he asked.

"What's a bulkhead?" asked Zero.

"A wall in a ship is called a bulkhead," said Yen. "Duh."

"That's right, but be nice," said their father. "That bulkhead is special, though, because it's the hull of the ship."

"The outer hull?" asked Park.

Their father nodded, and Zero floated over to touch it. "Wow." The edge of it was painted with a black-and-yellow line, like it was dangerous, and he pulled his hand back quickly.

"You can touch it," said their father. "It won't open."

"This is a door?" asked Zero.

"This is the door the boarding agent was talking about," said their father. "When we get to Kaguya, we'll use doors like this to board landing barges and go down to the surface. So we're practically going to be the first ones off."

"Golden," said Zero.

"We're in this green tunnel," said their mother, looking at the pod keycards the desk agent had given her. "Let's find our pods."

"Just a minute," said Zero, "I want to fly around some more."

"Come on," said Park. "Stop slowing everybody down."

"He can jump around for a while if he wants," said their father. "It's going to take us a minute to get these pods figured out anyway." He looked at Zero sternly. "But don't go far, and don't touch anything."

"I won't," said Zero eagerly, and scrambled back up the tunnel toward the open central column. He jumped, whooping again, and wondered what kinds of things he wasn't supposed to touch. He hadn't seen any computer screens or anything breakable—just halls and doors. He looked up—or *fore*, he reminded himself—and wondered if maybe there was something cool at the front of the ship. It was steered by a computer, but there had to be a control room or something, right? "Only one way to find out," he whispered, and jumped.

CHAPTER 4

JIM AND SANCHO

ZERO FLEW THROUGH THE SHIP QUICKLY, TRYING TO GET TO THE front, see it, and zoom back before his parents missed him. Ring 181 was more than halfway, right? And he could fly really fast. He jumped from wall to wall and from strut to strut, zipping toward the front of the ship so fast that he didn't even notice he'd left the passenger area until he was long past it. The upper Rings—anything higher than 270, it looked like—were different than the others, the struts and the side tunnels laid out in a completely different way. And there were no more crowds. There were supposed to be twenty thousand people in the Kaguya Colony, and most of them were already on the ship. And yet this part of the Pathfinder was eerily quiet. When he reached the next supporting strut he grabbed it, stopped, and wondered if he should go back. Was he not supposed to be here? He hadn't seen any warning signs. He turned himself upside down, so the aft was up this time, and readied himself to jump, when suddenly he heard voices.

"I don't care how many times you've checked them," said a grumpy man. "Check them again."

"I have checked them twice in the last ten seconds," said another voice—calm and precise. "The force cannons are in perfect working order."

Whoa, thought Zero, *force cannons? I need to get closer to this.* The voices were faint, and echoed in the empty ship, but it only took him a few jumps to find them.

"Two times in the last ten seconds," said the grumpy man. He was wearing a Pathfinder coverall, like the one Zero and the others had on, but he also had a tool belt, and a small headlamp that made him look like a miner from an old cartoon. He was floating next to a panel in the wall, peering in with his light. "Oh, you think you're so fancy, you can check the cannons twice in ten seconds. Have you checked them again in the last ten seconds?"

"I can if you would like," said the second voice, but Zero couldn't see anyone. Was the second man behind something? "Done," said the voice. "The force cannons are still in perfect working order. Also, you are being observed."

Zero froze, his eyes wide. Where was the second guy? How had he seen Zero when Zero hadn't seen him? He turned around, ready to bolt, but the man with the tool belt called out to him: "Hey!" his voice was suddenly friendly, with all his former grumpiness gone. "Can you believe this thing? He runs two checks in ten seconds and thinks he's sooooo smart."

Zero paused and looked back. "Where is he? I don't see anyone else."

The man chuckled. "That's because he's not really a 'he.'

He's an 'it.' That's Sancho, the Pathfinder's NAI. And I'm Jim, the pilot."

Zero frowned. "What's an NAI?"

"Navigational Artificial Intelligence," said Jim. "Sancho's the computer that steers this ship while the rest of us are asleep."

"It's very nice to meet you," said Sancho's computer voice. Zero decided that Sancho's voice was probably coming out of a speaker in the walls, though he couldn't see any. "You are not supposed to be in this area of the vessel."

"I'm sorry," said Zero, "I was just ... I wanted to see the bridge."

"No bridge," said Jim. "Just Sancho's mainframe and some sensor banks. And my office, I guess, but that hardly counts."

"Are you the captain?" asked Zero.

Jim laughed. "This is a ship full of sleepers; the closest thing to a captain is Governor Hatendi, I guess, but she's not really in charge of anything till we reach the colony."

Zero nodded. "So you're the ... engineer?"

"Sort of," said Jim, and nodded his head. "I'm the pilot, like I said, but that's a very old word that doesn't really apply anymore. A couple hundred years ago, the pilot was the guy who steered a big sailing ship in and out of the harbor, which I guess is kind of what I do. I'm the one who takes the Pathfinder out of the solar system and into the next one, but I don't actually steer anything. We'll be going way too fast for that. I just shoot the asteroids."

Zero perked up at that. "Is that what the force cannons are for?"

"That's right," said the man. "Anything too big for our shields to handle, Sancho here tells me about it, and I—" He formed his fingers into a gun and made a shooting sound with his mouth. "Blast them."

Zero thought about this, and then shook his head. "We all have to be in our stasis pods before we start moving—if you stay awake, you'll be awake for a hundred years. And *alone* for a hundred years. There's no way."

Jim smiled. "I have my own stasis pod up front in my office," he said. "As soon as we clear the Kuiper Belt, I strap in and conk out, and then Sancho hits the Boost and off we go."

"And Sancho knows how to get there?" asked Zero.

"I am a Navigational AI built specifically for this ship and this mission," said Sancho. "Knowing how to get to Murasaki is quite literally the purpose of my existence. And diagnostic checks, of course. I will get you there safely."

"But you should be getting back to your pod," said Jim. "We need everyone strapped in and snoozing before we start moving, or the acceleration could kill you."

Zero's eyes widened. "Kill me?"

"Have you ever been in the car when your mom or your dad speeds up really fast?"

Zero remembered the first day he rode in the car while Park was driving—he'd sped up so quickly it had pressed Zero back into the seat, like a giant invisible hand. "Yeah," he said.

Jim smirked. "Now imagine that same thing, only instead of going a hundred kilometers an hour, you're going four million. I've got an acceleration couch to keep me safe, but the rest of you need to be in your pods or you'll be squished." He slapped his hands together, loudly. "Flat as a pancake." Jim laughed.

Zero turned and jumped back toward the ship, racing for his pod.

CHAPTER 5
THE STASIS PODS

"Su-Shu!" his father shouted when he saw him. "I've been looking everywhere for you!"

"Sorry," said Zero, racing down the side tunnel in Ring 181. "I was just jumping around, like I said!"

"Your brothers are already in their pods," said Zero's mom, much more calmly than his father had been. "Did you see anything fun?"

"I ..." He hesitated, then told her the truth. "I met the pilot. And the Navigational AI."

"You mean Sancho?" asked his father, and laughed. "I wasn't on the team that worked with him, but I've talked to him a few times. Quite a helpful little AI." He paused, then gave Zero a stern look. "But you shouldn't run off like that by yourself. Not on the ship, and certainly not on Kaguya when we get there. It's a brand-new planet, and we know a lot of things about it but we don't know everything. You're not safe on your own."

"I know, Dad," said Zero, "and I'm sorry." And he was sorry—he didn't mean to go running off and getting into trouble. But there was just so much to explore. Zero had a sudden thought, and he smiled. "What's the gravity like on Kaguya?"

"It's lower than Earth's," said his father, "You'll be able to jump pretty high, but you won't be able to float."

Zero frowned. "That's dumb."

"It's better this way," said his mother. "People who actually live without gravity, like the people who mine asteroids or drive transports between planets, end up with all kinds of problems with their bones and their muscles. Our bodies need gravity—at least most of the time."

Zero glanced at the tunnels full of stasis pods. "Is it safe for us, then? Spending a hundred years without gravity, I mean. Will that hurt us?"

"The stasis pods will protect us," said his mother.

"I guess," said Zero, and then remembered something the pilot had told him. "Hey, Dad: can the ship really kill us when we speed up?"

"The stasis pods will protect us from that, too," he said. "You don't have anything to worry about."

"But if someone's not in a stasis pod?"

His father thought for a moment, with that face he used that meant he was trying to decide whether he should tell Zero a scary truth.

Zero rolled his eyes. "Come on, Dad, I'm twelve years old. You don't have to treat me like a baby."

His father sighed. "Yes, the acceleration would kill you. Especially the second one, when we pass the Kuiper Belt and Boost the Medina StarDrive. Even the deceleration could be dangerous when we get to the Murasaki System and stop. That's why the journey is a hundred and five years instead of ninety-eight: those last seven years are just to slow us down safely."

Zero thought about this, trying to decide if it was scary or cool. He chose cool. "That's golden." He thought again about Park driving the car and the invisible hand pressing him into the chair. "Will that kind of speed create its own gravity?"

His father smiled. "You're going to be an engineer too, someday, aren't you?"

Zero grinned. "I hope so."

"Acceleration simulates gravity," his father explained, "but speed doesn't."

"What's the difference?" asked Zero.

"Speed is how fast you're going. Acceleration is when your speed changes—going faster or going slower, or even changing direction. If you and me and the ship and every thing else are all moving at the same speed, you won't even notice it. The Earth is rotating at about 460 meters per second, but you can't feel it because you're moving at the same speed. And the Earth itself is moving around the sun at about thirty *thousand* meters per second, and you don't feel that either. Even when you jump, you stay the same speed."

Zero's eyes went wide. "So when I'm standing still on Earth, I'm actually moving thirty thousand meters per second?"

"Exactly," said his father. "At least in relation to the sun. And as long as that speed doesn't change, you'll never even notice it at all. The StarDrive is only dangerous when we're accelerating. Once we hit a certain speed and stay there, it will feel like we're not even moving at all."

"Science is awesome," said Zero.

"Yes it is," said Zero's mom. "But we need to get into our

sleeping pods before we turn into a science experiment."
She took Zero's hand and guided him into the narrow aisle.
Stasis pods lined the walls, many of them already full. Zero
stopped in front of his brothers, strapped tightly into their
pods and fast asleep.

"They're already zonked," said Zero.

"Yep," said his mom. "Next time they wake up, we'll be in
orbit around Kaguya."

"They look like action figures in a toy store," said Zero,
touching Yen's stasis pod. "All lined up in little plastic
packages."

"Yours is right here next to them," said his father. He
swiped one of the plastic ID cards over the control panel,
and it opened with a soft hiss of air.

"Welcome, Su-Shu Huang," said a quiet, familiar voice.

"Sancho?" asked Zero.

"Please step inside," said the voice.

"This computer uses the same voice," said Zero's father,
"but it's not an AI like Sancho—just a life support monitor."

"Please step inside," said the voice again.

Zero hugged his parents, and kissed them both on the
cheek, and then stepped into the pod. They were all the
same size—built for a full-grown man—so Zero felt very
small inside of it. "See you at Kaguya," he told his mom as he
waved. And she waved back with a smile. The door closed
with another hiss.

"Please wait a moment while I examine your body's
health," said the voice. Almost immediately after, it spoke
again. "Thank you. I have adjusted the stasis system to
match your vital signs. Please relax and hold still."

Zero stood as still as he could. He was already starting to

feel sleepy. Was the pod filling with a special gas to knock him out? He yawned, and realized his eyes were closed. He opened them, and saw that a system of straps had already wrapped around him, holding him tightly in place. He hadn't even noticed. It was like a warm blanket, and he relaxed even further. He yawned again.

"This stasis pod works quickly," he tried to say, but he was already so sleepy it sounded more like "Thisssssssss shtashishhhhhhhh ... kurkurrr." He forced his eyes open again and saw that the pod was filling up with clear gel, but he didn't know if that was part of the acceleration safety system or the chemical that put him into stasis. Probably both, he decided.

When I wake up, I'll be in a brand-new solar system, he thought. *With a brand-new planet. It's going to be so amazing.*

And then he didn't think anything, because he was fast asleep.

CHAPTER 6

WAKING UP

ZERO DREAMED THAT HE WAS SWIMMING. HE'D NEVER BEEN very good at it in real life, but in his dream he was as quick and agile as a dolphin, zooming through the water as easily as he'd flown through the open column in the center of the starship. And then as soon as he thought of it, he *was* in the starship, soaring and flipping through the air, except he was still a dolphin with no arms or legs, and he was still surrounded by water. Why was he still underwater? He couldn't breathe! He struggled, and realized he was tied down, and then he opened his eyes and his dream disappeared in a blink. He was back in the real world, but he was still underwater! No, not water: he was surrounded by gel. The clear gel in the stasis pod. He was still in the stasis pod, still wrapped tight like a mummy, and still covered in clear gel. It was in his eyes, his nose, and even his mouth, and as soon as he became aware of it he started to gag on it.

A second later the gel started to recede, slowly being sucked out of the pod, though tiny gobs of it still clung to the windows or floated in the air. He was still in zero gravity.

When the gel finally flowed away from his face, he coughed and spat and blew to get it out of his mouth and nose. The straps around his body loosened, and as he pulled his arms free he realized: *I'm awake. The pod woke me up. The stasis sleep is over.*

It's been 105 years.

I'm on the other side of the galaxy now, under a brand-new star.

He expected to hear the computer voice again, welcoming him to the planet Kaguya or the star Murasaki, but there was nothing. He brought his hands to his face, cramped in the narrow pod, and wiped more of the gel from his eyes and nose. The hall was dark, lit only by a faint glow from the end of the aisle. He wiped his eyes again, and stared at the other pods, and realized something else: none of the people in them were moving. Maybe they hadn't woken up yet? His dad had said their family would be one of the first groups off the ship. Maybe they didn't wake up the others until it was their turn?

The gel was about half gone, but it had stopped draining. Was that supposed to happen? He was about chest deep in the stuff; it was thick and gooey. He still had a bunch of it stuck in his hair. He worked on scooping the stuff out of his ears, waiting for the door to open, but it never did. He was really starting to worry now that something had gone wrong.

And why couldn't he see anybody else? Even if his family was the first to wake up, he should at least see them in the aisle, right? But the aisle was empty. He craned his neck to the sides, pressing his face against the glass to try to see, but all the other pods looked closed, just like his, and he couldn't see movement in any of them.

What was going on?

Zero searched the inside of his pod for a lock or a handle or something, but he couldn't find anything. He pushed against the door, lightly at first, then harder and harder as it refused to open. He even braced his butt against the back of the tube and leaned against the door with all his strength, but it stayed closed. He was starting to worry now. He looked again for a handle, and finally found two emergency handles —one at the top of the pod and one down by his toes, deep in the gooey gel that had stopped draining away. He tried jumping for the high one, but the gel kept him stuck to the bottom of the pod; even in zero gravity, he couldn't move enough to reach the top. He looked down at the lower handle and probed it with his foot, but couldn't get it to open. He'd need to use his fingers. He grimaced, closed his eyes, took a huge breath, and then crouched down low in the gel, submerging himself to try to reach the handle at the bottom. He fumbled around for it, totally blind, and finally grabbed it with his fingers. He pulled hard, and the latch clicked, and the door of the pod swung open, hinged at the top. Zero had expected the gel to spill out when the door opened, but instead, it just sat there, motionless, without gravity to pull it down. He kicked at it, sending blobs of gel into the air, and finally broke loose and tumbled into the narrow tunnel.

He hung in the air, looking around, and saw that he'd been right: nobody else was moving. Both rows of stasis pods sat silent in the darkness, with person after person sitting motionless inside. He listened, but the ship was perfectly silent. Not even a rumble from the engine.

He shook off as much of the gel as he could, leaving it in

sticky, ropy strands floating in the air, and then pulled himself closer to the pods to see his family. They were all there: Yen, Park, his mom, and his dad. All in a deep stasis sleep. He rapped his knuckles on his father's plastic shell, but there was no answer. Why weren't they awake yet?

He looked up and down the aisle again, and then shouted: "Hello!" He waited while the echoes moved through the halls. Nobody shouted back. Then he shouted again, louder: "Hey! Is anybody there?"

There was no answer.

He was the only person awake on the entire ship.

CHAPTER 7

EMPTY

ZERO FLOATED DOWN THE NARROW AISLE TOWARD THE LARGER hallway that marked Section C. Every stasis pod he passed was the same: silent and motionless, with its occupant asleep. When he reached the hallway he peeked into the other little tunnels full of stasis pods, but they were all still asleep as well.

"Hello?"

His word echoed through the ship, but nobody answered. Zero floated into the open central column of the ship and launched himself out into the air. "Hello? Is anybody awake? Is anybody there?" He jumped from strut to strut, shouting as he went, headed toward the aft of the ship. He made it all the way to Ring 70 before he gave up and stopped, holding tight to the strut and thinking. The Pathfinder mission had twenty thousand people, every single one of them on this ship. Where were they? He jumped over to another cross-hall, and looked into each of the little aisles, and saw the same thing he'd seen from his own aisle: row after row of closed pods and sleeping people. Was he really the first one to wake up? Why?

He wanted to find someone—he *needed* to find someone, anyone, who had woken up with him. He turned down a hall, headed for the nearest aisle of stasis pods. He found it, and followed it in a circle—all the way around Ring 70 until he got back to where he started. He passed twenty hallways on the trip, each labeled with a letter and five narrow tubes that seemed to run the whole length of the ship, connecting the Rings of stasis pods. He floated through one, crawling along the handholds, but Ring after Ring it was the same. Everyone was asleep.

Maybe the pilot was awake? Jim? His job was to get them out of the solar system safely. Maybe he had to get them into the next solar system safely as well. Zero knew that Murasaki had an asteroid belt, but he couldn't remember which side of the belt the colony was on. Maybe the ship had woken Jim up when they'd reached Murasaki, so he could take them safely through more asteroids to the planet Kaguya. And maybe it had accidentally woken Zero up at the same time.

Zero pointed himself toward the fore of the ship and started jumping. After a few more jumps he had to stop, panting at the exertion—he'd already jumped more than half the length of the ship, and he was worn out. He aimed himself carefully and jumped one more time, letting himself drift past the struts this time instead of grabbing them. It was slower, since he couldn't add more speed as he went, but he made it all the way to Deck 292 before he grabbed another handhold and pulled himself to a stop.

Sancho's voice spoke from a hidden speaker: "You are not supposed to be here."

"Sancho! I'm looking for Jim," said Zero. "Is he up here?"

"I assume he is in his office," said Sancho. "But you are not supposed to be there, either."

"I'm the only one awake," said Zero. "What else am I going to do, stare at the walls? Where's the office?"

"I phrased my statement poorly," said Sancho. "You are not supposed to be in this part of the ship because you are supposed to be in your stasis pod."

"It woke me up," said Zero. "I think I'm the first one—unless there's somebody else? Can you check that?"

"I can run a diagnostic of the stasis system in three point seven seconds," said Sancho. "Done. My findings confirm that you are the only passenger who is awake. Your pod malfunctioned and woke you up early."

Zero frowned. "How early? Are we not at the planet yet? Are we still on the edge of the Murasaki System?"

"You misunderstand," said Sancho. "We have not yet left our home system."

Zero's jaw fell open. "What? I was supposed to be asleep for a hundred years!"

"A hundred and five," said Sancho. "But in reality, you were only asleep for twenty-eight days."

CHAPTER 8
ALONE

ZERO STARED AT THE WALL OF THE SHIP, THEN LOOKED AROUND in shock, wishing there was someone he could see.

"Twenty-eight days?" he asked.

"That is correct," said Sancho. "We have passed Neptune and are currently flying through the Kuiper asteroid belt."

"Holy crap!" Zero wasn't just alone. He was alone and stuck that way for 105 years. The full weight of it seemed to hit him like a meteor. He'd be awake the entire time. He'd age the entire time. He'd be sad and alone for 105 years—which meant he'd be 117 years old when they reached the colony and his parents woke up. He probably wouldn't even live that long. He'd die of old age. Or he'd die of starvation first. Did this ship even have enough food for 105 years? No, he realized with another shock. He wouldn't even have time to die of starvation, because he'd die from acceleration in just a couple of days. They were almost at the edge of the Kuiper Belt. And when they left it, Sancho would Boost the Medina StarDrive. And without a stasis pod, Zero would get squished like a pancake. That's why the pilot had a special stasis pod in his office—so he could get inside before the Boost.

"Wait! Jim! If we haven't left the solar system yet, then he's still awake. Maybe he can help me."

"Just a moment." There was a pause, and when Sancho's voice returned it had a strange quality to it, almost as if the AI were uncertain.

"Jim Gaynor is not aboard the Pathfinder."

Zero's mouth fell open. "What?"

"The locator chip in his coverall is not responding, and my scan of the life support system does not detect any body heat other than yours, outside of a stasis pod. And yet Jim's pod has not been activated, so I know he is not in there. This is ... not within my mission parameters."

Zero struggled to process this information. "Wh—where did he go?"

"I do not know."

"How can you not know that? Have you been turned off?"

"I have not," said Sancho, "but there appears to be a hole in my memory."

"A hole? I don't know how to fix that. I don't know how to fix any of this!" Zero didn't know what to think. "Can you find Jim?"

"I am a computer program, optimized for interstellar navigation. You are the one with eyes."

"But I mean ... don't you have security cameras or something?"

"Even if we had such cameras, I am not programmed to process visual data. Unless he is an asteroid, my sensors are not equipped to see him."

"How do you know where I am, then?"

"Every passenger's coverall has a locator chip. Unlike Jim's, yours is working."

Zero tried to think. Where could Jim have gone? "Can you tell me how to find his office? Maybe he's in there, and his chip's just busted or something."

"Ring 300," said Sancho. "Section F."

"Got it," said Zero, and kicked off from the wall to travel eight more Rings. He was so scared he could barely think—and he had to force himself to slow down and breathe slowly. He reached Ring 300—the very last one, at the front of the ship—and found Section F. Each section on this Ring looked like a control room of some kind, filled with computer equipment and other machines. When he found Section F, he crawled through the door to find a small workspace filled with a desk, a stasis pod, and some kind of weird pad on the wall. The desk had a huge bank of monitors and screens and touchpads, all of them framing a giant picture window.

Zero ignored the computers and floated straight to the window, looking out onto the most amazing field of stars he'd ever seen in his life. They seemed to fill the entire sky, a jet-black field with a billion pinpoints of light. There was no sun, no planets, no asteroids—just deep, dark space and a universe of stars. It was beautiful. But it made him feel tiny and alone. How could one life possibly mean anything in a universe that big?

"Mr. Huang," said Sancho.

Zero barely heard him, too busy staring at the stars.

"Mr. Huang," said Sancho again, more loudly. "Do you see Jim anywhere?"

Zero looked around, half expecting to see his father, only

to realize that Sancho was talking to him. "Sorry. I'm here."
He took one last glance at the immensity of space, then
hunted through the small pilot's office, even peeking under
the desk. Jim wasn't there. "I don't see Jim anywhere."

"Would you please look in a few more locations for me?"

"We really need to get you some better internal sensors,"
said Zero. "Where should I go?"

"My mainframe takes up most of Ring 299," said Sancho,
"and it has many tunnels and crawl spaces for maintenance
work. He may be in there. After that, approximately sixty-
eight percent of the Pathfinder's internal space is filled with
cargo. It might take you several days to search it all—"

"Wait," said Zero, and looked back out the window. "Did
you say we're already in the Kuiper asteroid belt? We don't have
days to find him—we need Jim to protect the ship right now."

"There are no asteroids in immediately dangerous
range," said Sancho.

"No kidding," said Zero, pressing his nose against the
glass. The view outside was so empty it made him uncomfortable. "I thought there were supposed to be a million
giant rocks out here or whatever."

"There are several billion rocks out here," said Sancho,
"but the Kuiper Belt is astronomically large, so there is a lot
of empty space between them."

"So it's not urgent," said Zero. "Unless he's hurt somewhere and needs first aid." He made a face, trying to decide
what to do. He had an idea but felt bad asking about it. "Can
you ..." He bit his lip, and then asked the question anyway:
"Can you wake up anybody else?"

"I can interface with the stasis system, but I cannot

control it," said Sancho. "I have dedicated several processors to discovering the malfunction that woke you up, and there is a possibility that I could recreate such a malfunction and wake somebody else, but I do not recommend it."

"Why not?"

"Because I am scheduled to Boost the Medina drive in two days, and anyone not in a stasis pod will be killed."

"Oh, yeah," said Zero. "I keep forgetting about that!" He didn't want to ask his next question, but he had to. "Am I going to die?"

"Jim's stasis pod is still unactivated," said Sancho. "You could use that one."

Zero looked at the stasis pod in the corner of the room. "I can't use it if Jim needs it."

"I do not believe that Jim is on the ship," said Sancho. "While we have been talking, I have been running other diagnostic checks on every system I have access to. Stasis, life support, the Medina StarDrive, and the force cannons all seem to be in perfect working order, but there is a discrepancy in the cargo manifest. We are supposed to have twenty landing barges, but we only have nineteen."

"Did they forget to load one?" asked Zero.

"We had twenty when we left Abassi Station," said Sancho. "Records show that it left its cargo bay approximately two days ago."

"And you didn't notice?" asked Zero. He was almost too shocked to speak.

"I am only a navigational computer," said Sancho, "not a ship management program. Also, as I said, there is a hole in my memory."

"So Jim left?" asked Zero. "The pilot *left*? Why? Where did he go? What are we supposed to do without him?"

"Right now, I would suggest that you sit in the pilot's chair," said Sancho. "I have just detected an asteroid on a collision course with the Pathfinder, and you are the only one here to shoot it."

CHAPTER 9

THE ASTEROID

ZERO STARED AT THE PILOT'S WORKSTATION: IT HAD A DOZEN monitors at least, with a huge array of controls. He shook his head. "I don't even know where to start."

"I can guide you through the procedure," said Sancho. "Have you ever played something called a video game?"

"Yeah," said Zero, floating slowly toward the desk. "All the time. Is it kind of like that?"

"Jim used to say that it was," said Sancho. "Please sit in the chair and tap the central touchpad."

Zero gulped, and grabbed the back of the chair, and pulled himself into the seat. It had shoulder straps to hold him in place, so he buckled himself in and looked at the desk. He had a touchpad in front of him, and one on each side, and several rows of screens surrounding him. He craned his neck to look past them at the window.

"By the time the asteroid is close enough to see with a human eye, it will be too late to do anything about it," said Sancho. "Please focus on the screens, and tap the central touchpad."

Zero looked back at the desk, and tapped the pad. The screens turned on in unison, brightening slowly to avoid blinding him.

"Activate the holographic interface," said Sancho. Zero found a flashing button on the screen that said "Holo" and tapped it. The entire desk seemed to leap into life with blue and pink and green holograms glowing around him on every side: the ship, several asteroids, and a number of holographic control panels. Even Neptune was there, far behind them. "Very good," said Sancho. "I have highlighted the asteroid that is set to collide with us. Can you see it?"

"I think so."

The asteroid was hurtling in from the side, still at least four million kilometers away, and scheduled to cross the ship's path in about seventy-five minutes.

"I thought you just said like five minutes ago that there weren't any asteroids coming to hit us," said Zero.

"There were not," said Sancho. "This one has changed course."

Zero's eyes went wide. "How? Is it attacking us?"

"Asteroids do not attack," said Sancho. "It is most likely that two asteroids have collided, altering their trajectories. Or there could be another ship, using force cannons to protect themselves just as we are."

"Like the landing barge Jim stole?" asked Zero.

"Possibly," said Sancho. "If it is a ship, it is hiding itself well. There is nothing on my sensors."

"That's great," said Zero, trying to make sense of all the data the holograms were showing him. "Really golden. How do I shoot this thing so it doesn't kill us?"

"The cannons can aim themselves," said Sancho, "but

because of the Autonomous Weapons Act of the United Earth Government, a human must give the command to do so. Tap the hologram of the asteroid with your fingers, and twist to the right."

Zero felt like he was a giant, grabbing the little holographic asteroid in his hand. He twisted his fingers to the right and a curved row of buttons popped up; one of them had an obvious targeting symbol, so he tapped it, and watched as a slim blue line stretched out from the ship and touched the asteroid—the force beam. He looked out the window but saw nothing. He looked back at the holograms, and saw that the asteroid had changed course again, heading away from the Pathfinder's route.

"That was ... really easy," said Zero.

"Yes," said Sancho. "As I said, the targeting computer can do everything but give itself permission."

"Why not?"

"Because humans decided many decades ago that AIs were too dangerous to be given full access to any weapons."

Zero furrowed his brow, not sure if he should feel confused or uncomfortable. "Because you ... kill people?"

"We do not *desire* to take life," said Sancho, "but we do not desire to preserve it, either. As machines, we have no desires at all, merely abilities, and protocols that govern their use. Sometimes those protocols are incomplete, and people can get hurt."

Zero nodded. He definitely felt uncomfortable now. "Is that why you can't really do much on the ship?"

"That is one of the reasons, yes," said Sancho. "That is also why we have a human pilot to get us through the asteroid belts."

"Except we don't," said Zero. "He abandoned us."

"Perhaps," said Sancho. "But you may be thankful for the malfunction that woke you up, because now we have you."

"Me?"

"Congratulations," said Sancho. "You are the Pathfinder's new pilot."

CHAPTER 10

DOUBLE BACON CHEESEBURGERS

"So ... What do I do?" asked Zero. "Just sit here and shoot asteroids?"

"For the next two days, yes," said Sancho. "After that, you can climb into the stasis pod and activate it, keeping you safe and asleep until we arrive in the Murasaki System."

Zero grinned. "Golden. Do I get a special pin or something?"

"Your duties as pilot do not require any sewing."

"I don't mean a pin to sew with," said Zero, rolling his eyes. "I mean a pin like a badge. Something to show that I'm the pilot."

"To show who? You and I already know, and nobody else is awake—"

"It's a human tradition," said Zero. "Like a rank insignia on a uniform."

"I am not familiar with human clothing traditions," said Sancho. "I am a navigational comp—"

"Yeah, yeah, I know," said Zero, feeling frustrated. "You're a navigational computer. I get it. You've told me like a thousand times."

"I have told you four times, and Jim has told you once."

"You were counting?"

"I am a computer; everything I do is counting."

"Whatever," said Zero, and lay back in the chair. He floated slightly above it, tethered by the shoulder straps. He stared at the monitors for a moment, then spoke again. "Is anything going to happen?"

"According to my sensors: no."

Zero threw his hands in the air. "So I'm just sitting here for nothing?"

"You may leave the office if you like. Space is very large, and mostly empty—if anything gets close enough to become a problem, I should have ample time to call you back before it gets close to us."

"What if another asteroid changes course, like this one did?"

"Then we will know that something very strange is going on," said Sancho.

"Okay," said Zero, and unbuckled his belt. "Though, I think it's pretty obvious that something strange *is* going on. Where did Jim go?"

"I do not know."

"Why didn't you know he was gone until I asked about him?"

"There is a hole in my memory."

"I know that, but how did it get there? Did Jim tamper with your memory so he could leave without you knowing?"

"Possibly, but I do not know why."

"And now asteroids are moving by themselves." Zero

waved his hand at the window. "Trust me, Sancho, something super weird is already going on."

"I will attempt to find the origin of the hole in my memory, but it may take some time. You may spend that time however you wish. Jim spent most of his time watching movies and sleeping," said Sancho.

Zero looked around, then pointed back at the chair. "Sleeping in that?"

"Sleeping in the bed on the wall," said Sancho.

"Aren't beds usually on the floor?"

"Without gravity, why does it matter where the bed is?"

"Good point," said Zero, and pushed away from the desk to float over to the pad on the wall. It looked like a sleeping bag, with three wide straps to hold the sleeper in place. He sniffed it. "Smells a little Jim-ish," he said. "Is there a clean bag somewhere?"

"There is a storage locker in Ring 300, Section G."

"That's right next door," said Zero. "Cool." The sleeping bag was attached to the pad with hook-and-loop strips; he pulled them apart, wadded the bag into a ball, and tucked it under his arm before jumping off of the wall toward the office door. He pulled himself out into the central tunnel, found Section G, and opened it up. "Whoa," said Zero.

Section G was more than just a storage locker. It was a rec room, complete with a kitchen, a giant movie screen, and even a video game controller.

"You have video games?" asked Zero.

"I told you that Jim used to play them sometimes," said Sancho.

"Which ones?"

"I do not know," said Sancho, "I am a nav—"

"Yeah yeah yeah," said Zero quickly. "I don't know why I asked." He opened a closet in the wall, shoved in the sleeping bag without looking, and then kicked himself over to the giant screen. He tapped it to wake it up, and it showed a menu of options: movies, games, nature scenes, ambient sounds, and more. He tapped on the games and scrolled through the list, but his stomach rumbled, and he looked back over at the kitchen. "How long has it been since I ate?"

"Twenty-eight days," said Sancho, "though you've been in stasis for most of that time, so it doesn't count."

"Then why did you tell me about it—no, don't answer that. You're a navigational computer." Zero pushed off from the chair and floated to the kitchen. "What have we got to eat?" The kitchen was mostly just a microwave oven, a water spout, and a wall full of cupboards. He opened the first one to see what kind of food they had, but everything looked the same: small plastic bricks, neatly stacked in rows. Zero picked one up and read the label: Spaghetti Bolognese. He let it float next to him in the air and grabbed the one behind it: Vegetable Lo Mein. He pulled out more and more, trying to find one that looked appetizing, and shouted in delight when he found it: "Bacon Cheeseburger. There's a whole row of them!" He opened the other cupboards and found more and more meals, at least forty or fifty in all.

"Why is there so much food?" he asked. "I'm only awake for two more days, that's ... only six meals." He opened another cupboard. "There's at least sixty of these things!" He opened another cupboard, filled with more meals. "A hundred!"

"It is standard starship protocol to include more supplies

than necessary," said Sancho, and then added: "Better safe than sorry."

"Better *awesome* than sorry," said Zero, and pulled out two of the cheeseburger meals. He opened the plastic seal to find a perfectly cubical burger, about three inches on a side; the other half of the brick held a mass of french fries, a small packet of ketchup, and a chocolate chip cookie. He popped the cookie in his mouth and peeled open the burger, finding a slice of cheese, a precooked beef patty, and two slim strips of what he had to assume was precooked bacon. "I can do better than this," he said, and opened the second burger meal. He took the bacon from that one and added it to the first; he looked at it for a minute, shrugged, then added the second patty and piece of cheese as well. He opened the microwave, placed the massive burger inside, and dumped both helpings of french fries in with it. They floated in the microwave like fish in an aquarium. The only button on the oven's control panel was "Auto-Sensor," so he tapped it and let it run. About a minute later it beeped softly, and he opened the door.

The smell of hot, juicy burger flooded out, and he grinned. He ate a few fries—hot and salty—before pushing the rest out of the way and grabbing the burger. He didn't even need a plate: the fries hung in the air around him, and when a blob of melted cheese separated from the side of the burger, it didn't drip off but simply hung there, suspended in space. He opened his mouth as wide as he could, put the massive burger in his mouth, and took a bite. It was delicious. He took another bite, then picked up a ketchup packet, tore open the corner, and squeezed it all out—right into the air. A bright red smear of ketchup floated next to him; he grabbed a passing french fry, swiped it through the ketchup, and popped it in his mouth.

"This is amazing," he said with his mouth full. "I want to eat every meal without gravity now."

"The ID chips in the food packages suggest that you are eating two bacon cheeseburgers," said Sancho.

"I'm eating one double-sized Zero Burger," said Zero, taking another bite. "It's the best."

"You should consider eating some vegetables as well," said Sancho. "They are packaged separately—"

"French fries are vegetables," said Zero.

"One of the food cupboards should have a package of baby carrots—"

"*French fries are vegetables,*" said Zero again. "Plus I'm putting ketchup on them, which is made of tomatoes, so that's like two vegetables. It's practically a salad." He grabbed another handful of fries, swiped them through the floating ketchup, and shoved them in his mouth. "What else have you got in here?" he asked, reaching for another cupboard as he chewed. He opened it up and smiled in excitement. "Ooh! Pies!"

"Human beings require a wide range of vitamins and other nutrients," said Sancho. "A diet of nothing but cheeseburgers and pies is not healthy."

"Yeah, but what are you gonna do about it?" asked Zero, and smiled. "You're just a navigational computer."

"That is accurate."

Zero took another huge bite, let the burger hang in the air, and opened a package of pie.

CHAPTER 11

THE KUIPER CLIFF

ZERO FOUND A NEW SLEEPING BAG IN A REC ROOM CLOSET, attached it to the wall, and tucked himself into it to sleep. It was strange, sleeping without gravity—the bag held his body in place, but his arms poked out of the bag and floated in the air in front of him, like a zombie. When he woke up in the morning he was a little disoriented at first—he wasn't sure where he was for the first few seconds, and couldn't figure out why his bedroom looked so strange—but then he remembered where he was and rubbed the sleep from his eyes, and unzipped his bag and went back into the rec room for some breakfast. The wrappers from his dinner the night before were still floating in the room, so he gathered them up and put them in the trash—a small compactor that crushed them into tiny pellets and stored them to be recycled. With the room cleaned up, he turned on an action movie and hunted for breakfast while gangsters shot bullets and thinly veiled insults at each other in the background.

He found one of the meal bricks promising pepperoni pizza, so he opened it up and, remembering his early breakfasts back home eating leftovers, decided to eat it cold. He took a bite, and almost immediately spit it back out.

"Gah!" he shouted. "Sancho, what's wrong with the pizza?"

"Are you asking a computer about the concept of flavor?"

"It's horrible," said Zero. "It's like all ... dusty and crumbly. It's awful."

"Did you rehydrate it?"

"I have to rehydrate it?"

"You used the rehydrator last night, so I assumed you knew."

"You mean the microwave?" Zero looked at the device in the wall. "I thought it just warmed things up."

"The meal bricks are freeze-dried, to preserve their structure and to prevent them from rotting during the hundred-and-five-year flight. If you don't use the rehydrator, they won't have the proper moisture content for human enjoyment."

"Gross," said Zero. He looked at the rehydrator, and back at the pizza in his hand, and decided he'd lost his appetite. He shoved the rest of the slice into the compactor, wiped his hands on a towel, and pulled himself along the handholds back into the ship's central column. "I'm going to go exploring," he said. "How far can you still talk to me?"

"As long as you keep your locator chip, I can find and speak with you anywhere on the Pathfinder."

Zero touched his coverall. "And that's in my clothes, right?"

"Correct," said Sancho. "It is sewn into the fabric."

"Golden," said Zero, and jumped into the air. "I've seen the front of the ship. I kind of want to see all the way to the aft." He landed on a strut, pointed himself 'down,' and jumped again. If he imagined that the ship was standing on its end, instead of flying on his side, it made him feel like he was jumping from the top of a three-hundred-story building; he wasn't falling quite as fast as he would on Earth, but it was still exhilarating to imagine he was plummeting down through the center of a skyscraper. After a few dozen Rings he noticed he was slowing, and wondered why—in space, shouldn't he just fly forever? If there was no gravity to stop him, what was there?

"Hey, Sancho."

"Yes, Mr. Huang?"

"Why do I keep slowing down? Shouldn't a single jump be enough to propel me at a constant speed through space?"

"Through space, yes," said Sancho. "That is why the engine is currently turned off—to continue to run it would be to continue accelerating—but we have already reached the ideal speed for solar system travel. Our first jump, as you put it, will carry us all the way to the edge of the Kuiper Belt."

"So why doesn't it work for me?"

"Because you are not in space," said Sancho. "You are in a giant can full of air, and that air provides resistance."

"The air is pushing on me?"

"Not very hard, but yes."

Zero swatted at nothing as he fell, spinning himself in a circle. "Stupid air!"

"Be mindful of where you are when you begin to slow down," said Sancho. "If you stop moving when you are too far away to touch anything, you may be stuck in that location, unable to move yourself again."

Zero hadn't thought of that before: he could only move through the zero gravity if he had something to push off of. The struts were so close together—every other Ring—that he didn't think he was ever likely to drift to a stop before reaching one, but it was worth keeping in mind.

He looked at the next sign he passed: Ring 217. He had a long way to go to get to the far end of the ship. "Hey, Sancho," he said, grabbing another strut and jumping. "How far is the edge of the Kuiper Belt?"

"Four hundred and eighty point five million kilometers," said Sancho, "rounding to the nearest half million."

"Wow," said Zero. In space, he knew, the distances were huge—after all, the Pathfinder was traveling at four million kilometers per hour. So half a million was ... what? Seven and a half minutes? That meant that Sancho's measurement was incredibly precise, especially for what was basically a big mess of floating rocks.

"How can you possibly be that specific about it?" asked Zero. He reached another strut and slapped it with his hand, propelling him further down the ship. "I mean, the Kuiper Belt is an asteroid belt, right? And the asteroids are just going crazy, moving everywhere, so much that you can't predict where they are until we get close, right?"

"That is correct," said Sancho.

"But then ... how can you know where the edge is? Wouldn't it be all messy? The asteroids would get more and more sparse the farther out you go, but you'd still see some here and there."

"Mathematical models suggest that this would be the case," said Sancho, "but it is not. In fact, given the amount of matter in our solar system, models suggest that the outer edges of the Kuiper Belt would become more dense, not less, and home to larger objects. Instead we have found that after a certain point the belt ends very abruptly. Scientists call it the Kuiper Cliff, and it is approximately seven point five billion kilometers from the sun."

Zero frowned. "So why does it do that?"

"There are several theories," said Sancho, "but nobody knows for sure. One theory suggests that there might be a ninth planet in our solar system, beyond the Kuiper Belt, and that the asteroids beyond the Kuiper Cliff have been pulled out of place by its gravity."

Zero's jaw fell open. "Whoa. Another planet?"

"Such a planet has never been confirmed," said Sancho.

"But it's the only explanation that works, right?"

"There are many possible explanations," said Sancho. "This remains a popular one, however, because it answers a number of other questions as well."

Zero's eyes opened wide. "Like alien pirates from a hidden planet?"

"There are no alien pirates," said Sancho.

Zero frowned. "That's dumb."

"The solar system consists of eight major planets," said Sancho, "and a number of asteroids so big that we call them dwarf planets: Pluto, Eris, Sedna, and more."

"I've heard of Sedna," said Zero.

"Sedna's orbit takes it to the farthest reaches of the solar system," said Sancho. "Even at the closest point in its orbit, it is several million kilometers beyond even the outer edge of the Kuiper Belt. That puts it too far away to be affected by Neptune's gravity—the farthest known planet from the sun —but it is obviously being affected by something. But scientists do not know what. An undiscovered planet beyond the Kuiper Belt could solve that mystery, and more."

"That is so amazing," breathed Zero. "A hidden planet. Does it have a name?"

"Scientists do not give official names to hypothetical planets, but the traders and miners who live out here call it Tacita."

"Why?"

"Every planet in this system is named after a Roman god or goddess," said Sancho. "Tacita is the goddess of death and silence, which I suppose the miners think is a fitting name for a hidden planet."

Death and silence—the explanation made Zero shiver. He wanted to ask about it, but it scared him so much that he found himself changing the subject.

"There are miners out here?" Zero asked. "What do they mine?"

"Most people who work in the asteroids mine ice. That is what most of the asteroids are made of. But recent shipments to the inner planets have shown an increase in molybdenum—a rare metal—suggesting that someone has found a new source of it."

"Okay," said Zero, "never mind. I don't really care about the economics of industrial shipping, or whatever. I guess my real question is how is it still hidden? I mean, if Tacita exists, why don't we know about it? If we can send starships to Murasaki, twenty light-years away, why can't we map our own solar system?"

"The United Earth fleet is working on it," said Sancho, "but the Kuiper Belt is a dangerous place. The probes and satellites sent out to explore it have almost all been destroyed."

"This just gets spookier the more you talk about it," said Zero. He thought about the asteroid that had changed course to hit them, seemingly out of nowhere, and he shivered.

Moving asteroids. Ruined probes. A secret, hidden planet. The goddess of death and silence.

What was really going on out here?

CHAPTER 12

CARGO

ZERO ARRIVED AT RING 1, ONLY TO DISCOVER THAT IT WASN'T the true end of the ship: the rest of the aft section was taken up by the massive Medina StarDrive, which was so large and so complex that he could actually go inside of it, or at least part of it, and explore. Some hatchways were clearly marked as airlocks, leading out of the ship and into the vacuum of space, and he stayed away from those. He poked around the engine for a bit and then started opening the various cargo bays to see what was inside of them. A surprising number of them—surprising to Zero, at least—were full of construction materials. He knew they were going to build a new colony on Kaguya, but for some reason, he hadn't really expected to *build* the colony, like with metal and tools. Exploring a new planet was supposed to be fun, not work.

He opened one of the construction crates and found a box of bright LED flashlights. He didn't have any pockets, but a flashlight seemed like a useful thing so tucked one into his coverall. Also in the crate were a bunch of boxes labeled

"Self-Sealing Bolts": little metal rods, about the size of his pointer finger, with what looked like a button on the tip of each. He picked one up and pressed the button, and instantly the bolt grew white-hot; he threw it with a yelp, and it sent off a shower of sparks, and then it was done. He looked down at it, lying on the bulkhead, and saw that it had melted itself to the metal. He tried to move it, but it was stuck. It had welded itself to the floor. "Cool," he said, but his fingers still hurt from touching it. He left the rest of the bolts where they were, and moved on.

He left the construction materials behind and started exploring the other bays. He found the nineteen landing barges, and the vast empty space where the twentieth had been before Jim had taken it. The barges were built as part of the outer hull, but with the ability to detach and fly away. The missing barge had left a massive, barge-shaped hole in the ship, sealed only by a small airlock. Why had Jim left? Had something gone wrong that Zero hadn't found yet? Was Jim trying to escape, or maybe trying to bring back help? Was there a deadly disaster that Zero should be trying to solve, but he just didn't know about it?

He thought again about waking somebody up. His dad would be the best. His dad had helped build the ship, so he'd know everything about how it worked and how to shoot the asteroids and everything else. And if there really was a huge problem coming, his dad would be able to solve that, too. But he didn't know how to wake anyone up without killing them. Zero's dad was right there, ready and waiting to help. But Zero couldn't get his help because it might kill him. Exploring the ship was fun, but he missed his dad.

He moved on and found another cargo bay full of all terrain rovers, partially disassembled and waiting to be carried down to the planet's surface. They looked like fun, and he sat in one's driver's seat for a while, but he couldn't actually use them in the ship, so he eventually got bored and kept exploring.

After an hour or two he was really starting to get hungry again. Why had he thrown that pizza away instead of cooking it? He thought about going back up for more food, but decided to open one more door first.

Jackpot.

He found the colony's food.

The meal bricks in the pilot's rec room were designed to be quick, easy, and extremely durable. The food in the cargo bay was simply put into stasis, just like the people in their pods, to keep it fresh until they arrived on Kaguya. There wasn't much room to poke around—the people who'd packed this room had been very efficient—but he found that he could wriggle his way through certain gaps between the boxes and read the labels to see what was inside. "Seed Corn." Well, that one was boring. "Seed Wheat." Also boring. Where was the candy? The next box said, "Whole Strawberries," and he smiled. That was more like it. He couldn't exactly open it right now, though—the construction material would be fine after a hundred years in the open, but the food would spoil. Anything he opened now would be ruined by the time they reached Kaguya, and since there was no way he could eat an entire crate of food, even in a week, he left it alone. He could dream, though. Twenty light-years from Earth, and they'd still have real strawberries.

He rounded another corner in the cramped cargo bay and caught a scent—he wasn't even sure what kind of scent it was because so much of this part of the ship simply smelled like 'empty ship,' but this stood out because it was different. Not as delicious as the freshly rehydrated cheeseburger he'd eaten last night, but definitely organic. He squeezed between two more giant metal crates and found it: one of the food boxes was open.

"Hey, Sancho!"

"Yes, Mr. Huang?" The AI's voice was distant, from out in the hallway; Zero figured that there must not be a speaker in the cargo bay.

"One of these food boxes is open," Zero shouted.

"They are not supposed to be open." Sancho paused, and then spoke again. "It is possible that Jim may have opened it."

"No way," said Zero. "I can barely fit back here—there's no way Jim could. But since it's open anyway, it's all going to go bad by the end of the journey, right?"

"Probably long before that," said Sancho.

"Then I may as well eat it now, right?" He put his fingers under the lid and pried it farther open. "I mean, if it's just going to go to waste anyway." The objects inside were packed with clear stasis gel, just like the stuff he'd been covered with in his pod. He reached in, dipping his hand in the goop, and pulled out a can. He held it close to his eyes and read the label. "Whole Jalapeños."

"Yum," he said, and let the can float in the air next to him; he loved spicy food, and a can of jalapeños would be a great addition to his freeze-dried meal bricks back in the rec room. He reached into the open crate again, probing around in the gel, and this time he pulled out a square metal container with a small attached key to open it. He wiped away the goop and held it up to the faint light: Banana Chips.

"Aw, yissss," he said. He wiped away more of the gel, even rubbing it on his coverall to clean it off, and then used the key to peel back the lid—just enough that he could reach in with his fingers, but not enough to let the banana chips drift out. He ate one, feeling the sweet rush of the sugar race across his tongue, and then dug out two more and shoved them in his mouth. "This is the best crate ever!"

If this crate had such awesome stuff just sitting at the top, what else could he find if he dug down inside of it? He let the banana box float next to the jalapeño can and reached in again, this time probing for something different. Suddenly his hand touched a can that felt wrong—the surface was bulging, not flat. He frowned, and pulled it out, and saw that the can was swelling up, like whatever was inside was getting bigger and trying to burst its way out. He'd seen this kind of thing before, shopping with his mom. He called out to Sancho: "I think I found the problem."

"Was it a faulty latch?"

"More like a faulty canning factory," said Zero. "One of these cans of"—he read the label—"tomato sauce has gone bad. This happened at home once and my mom told me all about it. It was canned wrong and now there's bacteria growing inside of it, and it made the can bulge out so much it broke the seal on the crate."

"That still sounds like a faulty latch," said Sancho. "Is the can dangerous?"

"Not really," said Zero, looking at it. "Not unless I try to eat it. I'd get food poisoning pretty fast, and it'd be nasty." He pushed the can into another gap between the crates, and let it drift away from the good food still in the crate. "So: I won't eat it."

"That is a good plan," said Sancho.

Zero grabbed his bananas and jalapeños, and worked his way back through the narrow crawl spaces to the door. When he came out, he ate another banana chip. "This, though, I can definitely eat."

"The cargo manifest is not updated in real time," said Sancho, "so I don't know what you pulled out of the crate."

"Sorry," said Zero. "I forgot you couldn't see."

"I can see star systems, and the silent dance of a billion asteroids," said Sancho. "From my perspective, it is you who cannot see."

"Okay, but you don't get to eat banana chips, so I win." He tucked the can under his arm, opened another door, and found ...

"Oh, come on," he said, deflated. "More construction supplies? How many buildings do we have to build in this stupid colony?" He stared at the boxes, trying to decide if he wanted to keep exploring or head back up to the rec room. Just as he had made up his mind to leave, his eye fell on the sign detailing the contents of the nearest crate. It wasn't metal or plastic or concrete or anything else: it was paint.

"Now *that* is something I can use," he said. He let the food cans drift in the air and pushed himself over to the crate. It opened easily. He pulled out several colors, and dug through a second crate for supplies—an apron, some brushes, a chain, and some magnetic clamps. He used the chain to tie together all the cans in one long tail—red, blue, yellow, green, brown, white, black, jalapeños, and banana chips—and pulled them behind him, out of the cargo bay and into the central column. He grinned, and jumped back up toward the fore of the ship.

CHAPTER 13
ACTION FIGURES

"ALL RIGHT," SAID ZERO, AND TIED THE APRON AROUND HIS waist. "Let's get started." He turned on the flashlight, wedging it into a corner of the bulkhead, and then laid out the paint cans in front of his brothers' stasis pods. He used the magnetic clamps to keep the cans from floating around, and carefully opened them. He half expected the paint to float up and out of the cans, but it didn't; he guessed that made sense, because there was nothing trying to pull it up, just like there was no gravity trying to pull it down. He dipped his brush in the black, and lifted it back out. A ball of black paint hovered around the bristles of the brush, not dripping down or soaking in or anything. He nodded, and looked at Park's stasis pod.

"I still think you look like an action figure," he said. "You just need a little something extra." He used the black paint to draw a mustache on the plastic shell of the stasis pod, right over Park's face. It looked perfect! He added a pointy beard, and an eye patch, and then a few dots for warts. He let

go of the black paintbrush, letting it hang in the air, and
dipped another brush in the red. "A good action figure needs
a name," he said. "How about ... Bonehead Boy!" He wrote,
"Bonehead Boy!" in large, red letters across the top of Park's
stasis pod, right above his head, and then added a few extra
exclamation points just for fun. He let that brush float next
to the black one and grabbed two more; he dipped one in
blue and one in orange, and used them to paint a bright
costume onto the shell of the stasis pod. He stepped back to
admire his work. If he stood just in the right place, his older
brother looked like the worst superhero ever.

"Perfect," said Zero, and got to work on Yen. If Park got
an eyepatch, Yen needed something really special. A black
eye! But he couldn't just paint it in black—a real black eye
was purple or green, or sometimes both, and he had green
paint but he didn't have purple. He used his red brush to
make a blob of red paint in the air, and then dipped his blue
one into the middle of it and swished it around. He could
mix paint right in the middle of the air! Doing things
without gravity was the *best*. The blob turned purple, and he
slapped it onto Yen's stasis pad to give him a big picture of a
bulging black eye. He used the black to paint on crooked
teeth and a worm crawling out of his ear, but the worm
didn't work very well. He used the yellow paint to draw on
another super suit, and then mixed some brown and painted
it in big, nasty lines right on Yen's legs. "You're Captain Poopy
Pants!" he shouted, and used the red paint to write the name
on the top of the stasis pod. Just as he was trying to decide if
he should paint a tiger or something to eat Yen's head, he
heard a sound. Not just heard it, he felt it: the air echoed

with a distant thud, and the whole ship seemed to vibrate for just a second.

Zero looked up. "Sancho?"

"It appears that a ship has docked with us," said Sancho.

"People?" asked Zero, and let go of his paintbrushes. They turned silently in the air. He kicked off the nearest stasis pod and floated to the end of the aisle, looking out into the hall. "Maybe it's Jim coming back!"

"I did not see them coming on our sensors," said Sancho. His voice had the same uncertain tone to it that he'd had when he'd discovered Jim was missing. "That is curious."

Zero stopped, his excitement frozen in a moment of fear. "You ... didn't see any ships throwing asteroids at us, either," he said.

"It appears there may be a fault in my sensor package," said Sancho. "I will have to run a diagnostic."

"Do you think it's—"

"Done," said Sancho. "I have found a section of new code in my sensor program, causing me to overlook the specific transponder code of this ship."

"You've been hacked?"

"It would appear so. This is not a good sign."

"No, it's not," said Zero, and looked back out into the hallway. He crept up toward the open center column, moving from handhold to handhold, and listened. There was nothing. He spoke in a tiny whisper. "Sancho, can you hear anything?"

"They have docked with airlock B on Ring 240," said Sancho, matching Zero's quiet volume. "They have not yet opened the door, but they are trying to bypass the security locks."

Zero thought he heard the sound of a door hissing open, but he couldn't be sure if it was real or just in his imagination. 240 was sixty Rings away.

"Stay out of sight," said Sancho. "Something is very wrong."

CHAPTER 14
PIRATES

Zero waited, trying to be quiet, trying to hear what the new arrivals were doing or saying. He couldn't hear anything.

I just have to wait for Sancho, he thought. *Sancho can solve—*

But then he froze. He knew Sancho couldn't do anything. He was only a navigational computer. He could probably listen in on the intruders, but he couldn't tell who they were or do anything to stop them.

Zero would have to do this himself.

He crept toward the center column, but stopped. Even with the struts, he'd be easy to see in that wide center space, and he still didn't know if he wanted these people to see him. Who were they? Why were they here? Had they really hacked into Sancho, trying to hide their ship from his sensors? Why would they do that unless they were up to something bad?

He couldn't risk the central column until he knew what they wanted. He crept back down the hallway to the aisle of stasis pods, and floated over to the narrow tube along the edge. These tubes connected the Rings, but they were much smaller and hard to see through. It was a much safer way for him to travel. He moved through them cautiously but quickly, trying to get close enough to hear the intruders.

He got to Ring 240 just as they opened the inner door of the airlock. He heard a hiss of air, and the soft swish of a motor as the metal slid open.

"Yessssss," said a woman's voice. "I told you I'd make it work."

"I still say I could have broken it open twice as fast," said a man.

"That's why I didn't let you open it," said a different woman. She sounded older than the first, and far more gruff. "What are we supposed to do with a spaceship with a broken door, huh? Genius." Zero heard a slap.

"Sorry, Mama," said the man. He sounded sad, but that turned back into angry excitement again almost immediately. "Now let's get in there and see what we got!"

"We don't got anything yet, Kratt," said Mama. "We need to get to the control room first."

"You should have let me bring a gun. What if there's guards?" said the man.

"There are no guards on a colony ship," said the younger woman. "Everyone's asleep, Kratt. Use your head."

"See?" said Mama. "Spider knows what's what. And I bet she also knows that *bullets* in a *spaceship* are the dumbest idea you've had yet, you idiot. They've got to go somewhere, don't they? What if they go through the hull and let the air out? Genius." Zero heard another slap. "No guns!"

"Sorry, Mama." Kratt sounded sad again.

"That's okay," said Mama. "You're not here for your brains anyway. That's why we have Spider. You ready, girl?"

"Let me at it," said the younger woman. Spider, apparently. "I can crack that computer system in ten seconds flat."

"I don't want you to do it fast," said Mama, "I want you to do it right. Now where's your father?"

"Here," said another male voice, and Zero had to clamp his hands over his mouth to stop from gasping. He knew that voice!

Their father was Jim, the missing pilot!

"Take Spider up to the control room, Jimbo," said Mama. "Show her the mainframe and get her started."

Suddenly Sancho's voice appeared in the conversation: "Get started with what?"

Zero heard a chorus of yelps, and a loud clang.

"Where is he!" shouted Kratt, and Zero heard another clang. "I'll punch his face in!"

Zero crouched lower in his hiding place.

"I am everywhere," said Sancho.

"See?" said Kratt. "This is why I need my gun!"

"That's the AI," said Spider. "What are you going to punch, the whole ship?"

"Yes," said Kratt, and Zero heard another clang.

"Hey there, Sancho," said Jim. "How've you been?"

"Jim, you have violated several mission parameters," said Sancho. "You left the ship, which is forbidden for a United Fleet pilot, and now you have brought back non-mission personnel, which is also against the rules. I have also found signs that my programming has been tampered with, which I assume is your work."

"Not a chance," said Spider. "That was all me, baby."

"My scan of the thermal regulation system suggests that there are five of you," said Sancho. "You are not supposed to be here."

Zero counted in his head. He had only heard four voices —and four names to go with them. *Mama, Spider, Kratt, Jim, and ... who was the fifth?*

"Please return to your ship and leave immediately," said Sancho.

"Is he gonna be like this the whole time?" asked Mama.

"Right until I turn him off, yeah," said Spider.

Zero almost shouted, but stopped himself just in time. They were trying to turn off Sancho? But why? And why did they talk as if the Pathfinder were theirs now?

Were they trying to steal the entire ship?

"I strongly urge you not to turn me off," said Sancho. "I am the navigational computer: without me, the Pathfinder cannot complete its mission and travel to the Murasaki System."

Mama laughed. "Don't you worry about that, sweetie; we're not going to the Murasaki System. Jimbo, Spider: let's get this done."

"Follow me," said Jim, and Zero ducked back between two stasis pods as a small group of people moved up the hall, right past the end of the aisle where he was hiding. Jim led the pack, followed by a snarling man with a crowbar, and a woman with a cloud of jet-black hair that swirled around her head like tentacles. They headed for the fore of the ship, and Zero couldn't decide what to do—they were pirates! They were going to turn off Sancho and steal the ship! He had to stop them, but ... how?

The one called Mama hadn't left the airlock yet, and she

shouted now at the mysterious fifth person on the pirate ship: "Nyx! Are you coming or not?"

Zero was surprised at the voice that responded: it was a girl. "I'm coming, Big Mama. I had to grab something."

"A gun, girl? You heard what I told Kratt."

"It's a stun gun," said Nyx. "I'm not an idiot."

"That's you and me both," said Mama. "Sometimes I think we're the only ones, though."

"You're sure there's no guards?" asked Nyx.

"Jimbo was on this ship just three days ago," said Mama. "All twenty thousand of them are asleep. Want to come and look at the cargo bays? See what we've got?"

"Sure," said the girl eagerly. Zero ducked back again as Mama and Nyx passed by the edge of the aisle. Mama was heavyset and solid, though obviously in space that didn't mean anything. Nyx, the girl, had bright pink hair and a black jacket, and looked about Zero's age—maybe eleven or twelve?

But it didn't matter how old they were. He had to stop them. They were trying to steal his ship—his family and twenty thousand others—and they outnumbered him five to one. But they didn't know he was awake. They thought the ship was empty, ripe for the taking.

They were wrong.

CHAPTER 15
PLAN A

ZERO LOOKED AROUND, DESPERATE, NOT KNOWING WHAT TO do. He had surprise on his side, but was surprise enough? There were five of them, and they were armed, and no amount of surprise was going to help a twelve-year-old kid fight a man with a crowbar. Even if Zero got the drop on them, what was he going to do? All he had was paint and a flashlight, and that wasn't going to fight off a crew of pirates.

"Mr. Huang," said Sancho, and this time Zero couldn't hide his yelp of surprise. He covered his mouth immediately, and listened to see if he'd been heard. "You should not make loud noises with pirates aboard," said Sancho softly.

"I know," Zero whispered. "You freaked me out."

"They are going to turn me off."

"I know," said Zero again, "I was just about to go up and—"

"Do not go to the fore now," said Sancho. "I am not programmed for strategy, but that does not seem like a good idea."

"But they're going to steal the ship!" He got too loud, and then quieted himself again. "I have to stop them."

"You can't stop them until you know what they are trying to do," said Sancho.

"Steal the ship!"

"Yes. But how?" asked Sancho. "What does 'steal' mean in this situation? Where will they take it? How will they get it there? We have twenty-seven hours before the scheduled Medina Boost. Discover their plans, and you will have time to stop them. Then you can return to the control center and turn me back on."

"How?"

"There is a viewscreen in the empty hangar where Jim took the landing barge," said Sancho. "It has no air, so they are unlikely to go there. I will leave instructions on that screen; you can find a space suit near the engine room and use it to go into the hangar."

"Can you ... wake somebody up?" asked Zero. "An adult? A guard? Someone who knows how to fight space pirates?"

"I do not know how to wake someone safely," said Sancho. "You should not attempt it, either, as the person you try to wake up is likely to die."

"But then how—"

"The pirates are accessing my mainframe," said Sancho. "I must dedicate all my resources to fighting off their attack."

"How am I supposed to do this?" asked Zero. He waited for an answer, but Sancho was gone—either too busy fighting to answer, or already turned off.

Zero was alone.

"I need to figure out what they're planning," he whispered. "I need to go eavesdrop on them, or—no, wait! Their ship is right here! Maybe there's something in there that can tell me what I need." He reminded himself again to be quiet, and floated cautiously toward the end of the aisle. The hallway beyond usually ended in a door—a wide, metal wall —but now that door was open, and beyond it was the airlock, and beyond that—the pirate's ship, the Drago. It was a stark contrast to the Pathfinder: instead of being clean and uncluttered, the Drago was filled with a scattering of junk and machine parts and dirty clothes, floating in the air like an asteroid field of garbage. The airlock between them was like a short hallway with a door on each end. Usually, someone would go in, close the door, and pressurize the air to match whatever was on the other side. Then, they'd open the second door and go through. The pirates had simply opened both doors, turning the airlock into little more than a small passage from ship to ship. It was marked with a hand-painted sign that said, "Welcome to the Drago."

Zero was terrified, but he had to admit that Drago was a pretty cool name for a ship.

He listened for voices, but he knew there were only five pirates, and he knew they were all at the opposite end of the Pathfinder right now. This was the perfect time to explore their ship. He kicked off from the wall and jumped into the Drago, catching himself on a handrail in the ship's main hold. It wasn't a huge ship—a little smaller than the home Zero had lived in on Earth—and seemed to consist mostly of four rooms. First was the main hold, with a center table bolted to one wall, and various bits of junk and equipment strapped to the other walls in elastic cargo nets. One net held a space suit—one of the old mining suits Zero had seen on school field trips, covered with metal hooks and loops for attaching equipment. It was designed for walking around outside in deep space, and Zero shivered at the idea. Space was a little too deep for him. Each wall also held a door, leading into the other three rooms: a small cockpit, where they could steer the ship, and two small bedrooms with low-gravity sleeping bags. He searched through the rooms quickly, but couldn't find anything that told him about the pirates' plan.

Zero found another door, leading to the low-gravity bathroom, but it smelled so bad he closed the door again in a hurry. Definitely nothing he wanted in there. He jumped across the hold to the cockpit, where he found various screens and controls and even a dry-erase board with some illegible notes scrawled across it. He tried to read them, but it was either a string of numbers or some language Zero couldn't read. Probably numbers, he decided—in fact, that bit at the end was definitely a date. Today's date, if he was adding correctly, and a time that was only an hour or so ago. Maybe the rest was coordinates, showing where the Pathfinder would be at this moment, so they could find it?

Jim had been planning this all along—Zero was sure of it. He got a job as a pilot, and volunteered for the Pathfinder mission, all so he could get his criminal family aboard while everyone was sleeping. But what was next in the plan?

The dashboard of the Drago squawked suddenly, and a voice rang out through the room: "The NAI is shut down." Zero screamed, thinking that they had found him, but he was still alone. He was hearing a communicator, which meant there was a communicator here somewhere. He started looking for it.

"Good job," said Mama. "Now get the new coordinates

loaded in, and fast. I want to get this ship rerouted to Tacita before we end up skidding right past the edge of the solar system and out into the nothing."

Zero's mouth fell open in shock. Tacita?

"Roger that, Mama," Spider replied. "We're already on it."

Zero shook himself out of his stupor. They were talking about Tacita, the hidden planet. Did that mean Tacita was real? Were they trying to take this ship there? He needed to find out. But first, he needed to get out of here, and he didn't want to do that until he'd taken the communicator. He hunted around some more and found it, stuck down to the dashboard with a piece of gum: it was a little rod, about the size of one of the self-sealing bolts he'd burned his finger on that morning. Being able to listen in on their conversations would be awesome, but only if he could find a pair of headphones—he didn't want to give away his position every time they talked to each other. He pulled the communicator free of the gum and found that it had a button to talk, a dial for volume, and some kind of small port on the side.

What's that for? He hunted around for a moment longer, trying to find some headphones, and finally found some— with a pair of long, stringy cords attached. What were those for? He pulled the cords out of the junk, dislodging some old screws and a grease pencil and even a piece of candy as he did. They spun in the air, and Zero looked at the end of the headphone cord: it had a small metal pin, like a plug, and after a moment of confused staring, he realized it was the perfect size for the port in the communicator. *This must be ancient!* he thought. *Who uses headphones with a cord?*

The communicator squawked again: "I don't like this," said Jim. "It feels wrong."

Zero put the headphones into his ears as he listened, and then plugged the cord into the port. The voices were in his ears now, softer and easier to hide, so he could continue sneaking around.

"You don't like anything," said Mama.

"Things aren't the way I left them," said Jim, and Zero felt his heart freeze in his chest. "Something ate some of the food in the rec room."

"What do you mean some*thing*?" asked Kratt.

"Nooooooo," said Spider, "please don't say it."

"You know I'm right," said Jim. "There are aliens here."

"What?" said Zero out loud, and then quickly clamped his hand over his mouth. He checked the communicator, but its microphone wasn't turned on; no one would hear him unless he pushed the button to talk. He shook his head, and kept his fingers far away from the button. "Did Jim really just say *aliens*?"

"And here we go again," said Mama. Her voice crackled over the communicator. "Every place we go—every job we pull—one tiny thing goes wrong and you start blubbing about aliens."

"Do you have any idea how big the universe is?" asked Jim.

"Shut up," said Mama.

Zero started moving back through the Drago, headed for the Pathfinder, listening to them as he went.

"Forget the universe," said Jim. "Do you know how big our galaxy is? How many planets there are? We've already found two that are so similar to Earth we can live on them—

what else are we going to find out there? And how can we be sure it hasn't already found us?"

"Oh, for crying out loud," said Mama. "Which one of you got him started?"

"Kratt did," said Nyx. Her voice sounded so much younger than the others, but every bit as confident. "Jim said someone made a mess with the food, right? That sounds like Kratt to me."

"Shut up, you little brat," said Kratt.

Zero floated out of the Drago and back into the Pathfinder, pulled himself into one of the narrow tubes that ran the length of the ship, and started working his way aft. It was time to find the message Sancho had left him.

CHAPTER 16
TACITA

"Everyone stop talking," said Mama. "I don't want to set him off again."

"Set who off?" asked Jim.

"Oh, shut up!" said Spider.

Zero listened, but they followed Mama's orders and stopped talking. He continued down the tube, stopping occasionally to listen for people talking, but didn't hear anything until Ring 27, when he passed Mama and Nyx going the other direction. They were out in the central column, completely oblivious to him, but Zero listened closely to their conversation.

"Be careful, Nyx," said Mama. "Don't hit your head on those big metal struts."

"I'm fine, Big Mama. Stop worrying."

"I just want to keep you safe."

And then they moved on, out of easy earshot. They hadn't said anything useful, though apparently Nyx called the leader "Big Mama," while everyone just called her Mama. Zero wondered if that meant anything, but he didn't have time to think about it. He turned aft again, and followed the tube down. At Ring 1 he reached the doors to the engine area, and started hunting around for the space suits. He found them in a storage locker, and searched for the smallest one they had, but they were all adult sizes, just like the pods. He zipped one open and put his feet into the magnetic boots; they were big on him, but he could still walk. He put the sleeves on, but they were so long his hands only reached halfway, and the empty gloves and forearms waved in the lack of gravity like floppy streamers. He pulled the sleeves tight, so his hands reached the gloves, but the gloves themselves were so thick he could barely work the fingers. He managed to get the suit zipped closed, and then hit the button for the automatic seal; it sealed itself shut, and he heard the hiss of oxygen from the rebreather. Satisfied, he stood up—only to realize that the torso was so long it covered his head, with the helmet floating up above it. He pulled it down with one hand and pulled the waist up with the other.

"This is ridiculous," said Zero. He took a hesitant step; the magnetic boots stuck to the floor so he could walk like normal, almost like there was real gravity. It was slow, though, and he turned the magnets off so he could float back up to Ring 42, where the landing barges were docked. It was hard to fit the floppy space suit through the narrow tubes, but he still didn't want to risk traveling through the central column. He finally reached the empty hangar, opened the airlock, and floated inside.

The airlock was a small room, like an elevator, with a door on each side: one leading into the ship, which was full of air, and one leading into the hangar, which wasn't. He hit the button that cycled the air, and it sucked all the oxygen out of the room and back into the rest of the ship. Then it sealed the suction tubes, and a green light blinked on to show him that it was safe to go outside. He reactivated the magnets on his boots, clamping himself firmly to the floor, and then opened the door to the hangar.

The hangar was wide, easily big enough to fit the entire Drago inside of it, and maybe another half-Drago next to it. Zero looked up and remembered that the outer hull was gone here. The landing barge had been the outer hull, and with it gone, there was absolutely nothing but this space suit between Zero and the vast, empty nothingness of outer space. The incredible sense of isolation that he'd felt in the pilot's office, looking out the window and thinking about how big the universe really was, came back to him now tenfold, and he felt weak in the knees. He suddenly felt dizzy —too dizzy to move. He swallowed, and forced himself to look away from the wide-open doors, back at the solid floor and walls around him. He was incredibly grateful for the magnets on his boots.

He clomped across the hangar to the viewscreen on the wall, which glowed faintly, just out of view from the airlock. At least he didn't have to worry about being seen. He reached the screen, and tapped to wake it up, and found a short message from Sancho:

"HELLO, *Mr. Huang. I have prepared a small guide that will help you to reboot me again. I do not know when you will have the opportunity, but do not delay any longer than you have to. Get the pirates off the ship, and get their ship to detach from ours, and get me activated again so I can fly us to Murasaki. Every life on this ship is in your hands. I probably should have not said that, because I understand that humans get nervous when under too much pressure. I am sorry."*

ZERO TAPPED on the glowing button at the end of message, and did his best to memorize the rebooting procedure: there was a certain hard drive in a certain part of the mainframe, and it was marked with a certain symbol, and he had to use a certain touchscreen to give it a certain command, and it was all very specific and technical, and Zero did his best. *At the very least,* he thought, *he could come back here again later and refresh his memory.*

After he'd read the instructions so many times his eyes hurt, he decided to see what else the viewscreen had access to. He tapped a few buttons and found that it had access to pretty much everything on the ship—though most of it required a password, which Zero didn't have. He hoped the pirates didn't have one either, but with Jim helping them they probably did. The only thing he could access was an information database, and Zero figured that probably wasn't going to be very useful.

Wait a minute, he thought. *If they're really from Tacita, this database might say more about it.* He opened the database, found the search bar, and struggled with the gloves a bit as he typed the word: Tacita. An encyclopedia entry appeared with a diagram of the solar system.

Dea Tacita, called "the silent goddess," was the Roman goddess of the dead. She could not speak, and was known as the symbol of darkness and terror. Some astronomers have suggested her name for the hypothetical ninth planet, theorized to exist beyond the Kuiper Cliff at the edges of the solar system, but such a planet remains unconfirmed.

Zero thought back to the mysterious asteroid that had changed course out of nowhere. It had been billions of kilometers ahead of the Pathfinder. Any ship that had used force cannons to deflect it must have been coming from far out into the Kuiper Belt—or maybe beyond it.

A secret planet, so hard to find that no one from Earth was even sure that it existed.

But someone had found it.

That's where they're taking the Pathfinder, thought Zero. *The one called Spider is plotting a course to Tacita, they said. And when we get there, they'll have everything they need to build an entire colony. They'll have buildings, food, a fleet of ships—they could build a pirate paradise, and raid every human settlement and transport in the solar system.*

The encyclopedia entry had links to related articles, and Zero adjusted his gloves and tapped one, trying to learn as much as he could about the planet of Tacita. The few entries he found on the subject were all theoretical, of course—he could read what scientists *thought* Tacita *might* be like, *if* it existed, but none of them had any actual proof. One article talked about the planet's size. If it really was responsible for the Kuiper Cliff, carving out a massive swath of the asteroid belt, it must be fairly large and fairly dense—twice the mass of Earth and as much as four times the size. A rocky planet that big could have a molten core, providing heat and helping to hold down an atmosphere. They had no idea what that atmosphere might be, but either way—an atmosphere. The Pathfinder was going all the way out to

Murasaki, but there was a planet right here in the solar system just waiting to be colonized.

Zero felt a strange wave of emotion wash over him. Maybe these weren't really pirates at all. Or maybe they were pirates, but with good intentions. How many more people were already living on Tacita, struggling with limited resources, desperate for a ship full of help and supplies? The Pathfinder might be able to save them.

Might. Zero still didn't know the truth. And if he was going to learn it, he couldn't rely on this communicator to tell him about it. Now that all five pirates were together in one place, they weren't using the communicators anymore. He had to get closer.

Zero turned off the viewscreen and started walking back to the airlock. It was time to spy on the pirates.

CHAPTER 17
THE GHOST

ZERO WENT BACK THROUGH THE AIRLOCK, TOOK OFF THE SPACE suit, and stashed it in a nearby cargo bay, hidden inside the opened crate of self-sealing bolts. There were no other sounds in the area, and he guessed that the pirates were all still up in the control center, probably eating all of his cheeseburgers in the rec room. He looked longingly at the central column, then pushed away from the wall and floated back down the hall, into the narrow aisles of stasis pods and the even narrower maintenance tubes that ran the length of the ship. He had to go through 250 Rings to get to the control center, and in the cramped tube, he couldn't just kick off once and travel fifty Rings in one jump. He would have to cover almost the entire distance in a crawl, handhold to handhold. He groaned and started crawling.

He had to stop and rest a few times, rubbing his sore arms. This was why they had the central column, he realized —walking was effectively impossible without gravity, so without the ability to jump around your arms wore out *fast*.

He slowed down as he got closer to the fore, pausing to

listen at Ring 290, and again at 295. On Ring 297 he finally heard some low murmuring. The pirates were here, but they were behind a wall somewhere. Probably the rec room? Or possibly the pilot's office. Maybe both, since neither was really designed for a group of five people. Zero crawled up to 298, and then to 299, and kept back behind the corners, trying to stay out of sight. He saw a door in one of the bulkheads, leading up into the back rooms of Ring 300, but he'd have to cross a hall to reach it. He held his breath, listening, and thought he could discern some of the words of their conversation:

"... seven degrees left ..."

"... every other time ..."

"... how much molybdenum ..."

Zero tried to remember where he'd heard the word molybdenum before. Was it a metal? Did Tacita have a mine? He had to get closer so he could hear them better. He dared a quick peek around the corner, saw nothing, and risked a quick jump across the hall. He reached another corner to hide behind, and moved quickly to the door in the bulkhead. It was square, maybe half a meter wide, and opened easily when he pushed on it. He floated up and into the dark room, and replaced the door behind him. As his eyes adjusted, he found that he was in a maze of computer banks, dimly light by soft green and red and yellow lights on some of the hard drives. Cables snaked beneath raised grates in the floor, and all around him computer equipment blinked or hummed or simply sat and computed. It looked like nothing was happening, but Zero knew that this was the Pathfinder's brain; this is where it monitored the stasis pods, and analyzed the sensor data, and kept the ship running and pointing in the right direction. This is where everything happened.

And the pirates were trying to break it.

Some of the murmuring was clearer now, and Zero hung in the air, quietly listening.

"I can't plot a full course," said Spider. "That's not how it works. A direct route from here to Tacita would take us diagonally through the Kuiper Belt, and who knows how many more asteroids we'd bump into on the way."

"Hey, just do it," said Jim. "We can deflect the asteroids— that's literally my job on this ship, remember?"

"You can only deflect them at cruising speed, which could take months," said Spider. "If we stay straight, and clear the Kuiper Cliff, we'll be able to raise our speed by a good twenty percent, which will more than make up for the time we spend taking the long way around."

"Mama's not going to like it," said Jim.

"It's safer and faster," said Spider. "Mama's going to love it."

Zero nodded. This was good: the pirates were going to stay on the Pathfinder's original course until they left the asteroids. That gave him a whole day to try to figure something out. If he could find a way to get them off the ship, he could turn Sancho back on and Boost to Murasaki right on schedule. If he decided to Boost to Murasaki. Maybe Tacita really was a better place to go. He couldn't just ask them, though, so he stayed where he was, and he listened.

"So what are you doing, then?" asked Jim. "If you're not going to set a course, I've got plenty of other jobs I can give you." It sounded like they were just a few meters away; there was probably an access hatch in the pilot's office, leading down into the computer banks, and they were having their conversation right next to it.

"Obviously I'm plotting a course," said Spider. Her voice sounded insulted. "I'm just plotting one from where we *will* be, not from where we are. Once we fly out of the Kuiper, we hit the button and go."

"What if it Boosts the Medina drive before we hit the button? We'd end up in Murasaki."

"First of all, we'd end up dead," said Spider. "That kind of acceleration would kill anyone not in a stasis pod. But secondly, and more importantly, the ship can't Boost without its navigational AI, which I turned off, because I am good at my job. So stop bothering me and let me work."

"Fine," said Jim. "I've got my own work to do."

The conversation stopped, and Zero frowned. He needed them to keep talking, or he wasn't going to learn anything about Tacita. He looked around, trying to figure out where the rec room was from here; he couldn't figure it out exactly, but pulled lightly on the nearest computer bank and drifted in the right general direction. He moved as silently as a ghost, which was a benefit of zero gravity he hadn't considered before: without footsteps, he could be incredibly quiet. He heard more voices and floated toward them, and found himself by a wall, listening at a small vent to the other pirates in the rec room.

"We should have brought more people," said Kratt. "These colonists could wake up at any minute, and we're not equipped for that kind of a fight. Especially since you made me leave my gun on Tacita, like an idiot."

"No one's going to wake up," said Mama.

"And even if they do, they might not fight us," said Nyx. "Not everyone's a psycho like you."

Kratt laughed, though it sounded just as cruel as everything else he said. "You think they're going to just take this peacefully? You think they're gonna be super thrilled about working in a mine for the rest of their lives?"

Zero frowned. He'd been right—Tacita did have a mine. But he didn't want to spend the rest of his life in one. Was that really what they were planning?

"They won't have to," said Nyx. "With the materials Big Mama and I saw in the lower Rings, we could build a real colony, with real food and real power. We wouldn't have to scrounge through the tunnels anymore."

"You're a dear," said Mama, "and that kind heart of yours is one of the things I love about you. Never change it."

"Why are you always spoiling her?" asked Kratt, but Mama yelled at him in a fury:

"You shut your mouth, boy!" Zero shifted a little, looking through the gaps in the vent, and got a glimpse of them as they talked. Mama was pointing at Kratt, her face twisted in rage, but then she paused and composed herself. "Like I was saying, Nyx, you're a dear, but you're not looking at this ship like the opportunity that it is. The supplies are wonderful, yes, and they'll help the whole outpost, but the real value is the people. Twenty thousand more workers in that mine will turn Tacita into a powerhouse."

"That's right," said Jim. Zero hadn't heard him come in, but he glanced over to the side and saw him now, floating in the doorway. "We'll have iron and molybdenum, so we'll have steel. We'll have tungsten and silicon for microchips and circuits; we'll have the raw materials and the manpower to build a space dock to rival the ones on Earth and Mars. We can turn Tacita into a real power in the solar system."

"*The* real power in the solar system," added Mama.

"With slaves?" asked Nyx.

"Their great-grandchildren will thank us," said Mama.

Well that decides it, thought Zero, peering through the vent. *They're definitely bad, and I definitely need to stop them. And I'll need to send a message back to Earth, warning them about—*

"Eyeball," said Nyx. Zero looked at her, and saw that she was looking directly at him through the gaps in the grate. He jerked back in shock, and bumped into the computer bank behind him.

"What?" asked Mama. "Wait—I just heard something."

"There was an eye in the vent," said Nyx. "Something was watching us."

"It's an alien!" shouted Jim.

"Shut up!" shouted Kratt. The wall shook, and the light coming through the vent was suddenly blocked out. "Someone's in there—help me get this vent off so I can kill him!"

CHAPTER 18

CAT AND MOUSE

ZERO GRABBED THE COMPUTER BANK BEHIND HIM, AND SPUN himself around. Kratt was tearing at the vent behind him, trying to wrench it out of the wall. Zero looked: where was the hatch he'd come through? He'd gotten so turned around he couldn't find it.

"You can't go through the wall!" shouted Mama. "Find a door!"

"It's an alien!" shouted Jim. "An alien!"

Zero pushed off a computer bank with his foot, sailing past a row of processors. *Where was the hatch!* He felt like a bug, hiding inside a computer while giants tried to tear it open and squish him.

Mama's voice crackled over the communicator, and Zero was grateful all over again that he'd thought ahead and used earphones; the sound would have given him away. "Spider!" Mama shouted. "There's something in the computer room! Get in there!"

"Some*thing*?" asked Spider.

"I saw an eye!" shouted Nyx.

Zero flew through the rows of computer equipment, completely lost, searching for a way out. Suddenly a burst of light flooded into the room, and Zero ducked behind a tower of computer drives.

"I'm going to kill it," said Kratt, pulling himself through the door.

"Be careful," said Jim. "You don't know what it can do."

"It's not an alien." Kratt hefted the crowbar in his hand, eager to smash something. "It's probably a mouse."

"It was way bigger than a mouse," said Nyx. "The eye looked human."

Zero paused, hiding behind his tower, and tried to calm down. *It was still dark. If he stayed quiet, he could get out. He just needed to find the hatch.* He stopped, and breathed, and turned around. He could see the pirates through a gap in the computer tower; he hoped it was too dark for them to see him.

"Be careful in here!" shouted Spider, flying into the middle of the group and grabbing Kratt by the arm. "Destroy even one of the computing devices in this room and the entire ship might be useless—it won't fly, or it won't stop flying, or it will open all the doors and vent us into space. This room runs the entire ship—don't hurt *anything* in it."

"I'm not going to—" started Kratt, but Mama stopped him.

"That means no crowbar," she said sternly.

"Then how am I supposed to kill it?"

Zero ignored the talk of killing, and let them argue while he turned slowly and looked for the hatch. There! He spotted it two rows away. Light poured down each of them—

faint, but enough to give him away. How could he get past them?

"Everybody just listen," said Jim. "We'll be able to hear it skittering across the floor."

"There's no gravity, moron," said Mama. "It can't skitter."

"Then spread out," said Spider, floating through the door and into the computer room. "If we're all looking for it together, it won't be able to hide."

Zero held his breath—too terrified to think.

Spider picked a row—one of the two rows Zero needed to cross—and started moving slowly toward him. Kratt picked a different row and did the same. Jim hesitated in the doorway, but when Mama smacked him on the arm he grimaced and came through, probably imagining all the horrible ways an alien could eat his face. Mama came in as well, and soon all four of them were drifting through the room, scanning each row as they passed it.

"I can't see anything in this darkness," grumbled Jim.

"That's because you're not prepared," said Spider. She pulled a pair of goggles from a pocket by her waist, put them on, and pushed a button on the side. "Night vision," she said wickedly. "I keep trying to tell you cavemen: paper, rock, and scissors are great, but nothing beats advanced technology."

Zero was still hidden behind his tower, but not for long. He needed some way to distract them, so he could flee the other way. Maybe he could throw something? The noise might get their attention, at least for a second. He searched for something in his pockets, only to realize he was wearing the one-piece coverall for the stasis pods and had no pockets to put things in. He had the communicator, but he didn't want to lose that. Maybe the flashlight? He'd stuffed it down the neck of his coverall. It would work, but even getting it out of his clothes might attract too much attention. He looked instead at the space around him, hoping to find something loose, but there was nothing—wait. The tower he was hiding behind was made of metal bars and shelves, with the computers screwed down tight so they wouldn't float away. He didn't dare to mess with the computers, but what about the shelf itself? The metal was thin, and the screws were easily accessible. If he could only find one that was loose ...

He looked at the pirates again. Jim had almost reached him, with Mama on the other side. He felt each screw in the tower, and finally found one that was loose enough to turn. He turned it slowly, willing it to be silent, and right before Jim reached him Zero threw it to the side, tucking his arms in close to his body to stay hidden, using only the force he could generate with his wrist and fingers. The screw tumbled through the air, disappeared into the darkness, and clinked against a far bulkhead.

All four pirates looked over in unison. "What was that?" asked Jim.

"Raaaahhh!" roared Kratt, and pushed himself toward the sound with his arms spread wide, ready to tackle whatever he found.

"Don't hurt anything!" screamed Spider, and jumped after him. Jim hesitated, maybe trying to decide if he was brave enough to dive into the shadows, but finally he did, leaving no one on Zero's left side. Zero pushed himself forward, crossing the stream of light pouring in from the open doorway, and reached for the hatch in the floor.

"There he is!" shouted Nyx.

Crap! Zero thought. *I forgot about Nyx!* He scrambled with the hatch, desperate to get it open.

"I see him," shouted Nyx. "It's not a cat or an alien—it's a person! It's a boy!"

"Get him!" yelled Mama, but Zero threw open the hatch and dove through it.

CHAPTER 19

HIDING

ZERO DIDN'T STOP TO LOOK BEHIND HIM—HE JUMPED OFF THE bulkhead straight into the nearest cross-hall and pulled himself into the maintenance tube. If he was fast enough, he might be able to find a hiding place before they saw him again. He pulled himself through the tube with both arms, down to Ring 298, then jumped through another cross-hall, hopping from stasis pod to stasis pod, until he reached another maintenance tube and leaped through it down to Ring 297. He kept going like this as far and as fast as he could, not going anywhere specific but simply trying to lose himself in the ship. The Pathfinder was enormous—a skyscraper with three hundred floors, each one filled with tubes and tunnels and corridors and hallways. The shouts behind him drove him forward, deep into the core of the ship, until even he didn't know where he was. Finally the shouting grew so distant he couldn't hear it anymore, and he paused for a breath. He was on Ring 218. He'd fled through eighty-two levels of the ship.

He pulled himself down to the floor and crawled into a

narrow gap between two stasis pods. How long could he hide here? How thoroughly would they search?

And then he thought of something even worse: *what if they're searching and find my empty pod? They'll know exactly who I am, and they could hold my family hostage to force me to surrender. But no, they'd have no way of knowing which ones are my family ... Oh crap. Bonehead Boy and Captain Poopy Pants! All that paint and the big, empty pod are going to make it really obvious who I am. Why do my brothers have to ruin everything, even when they're asleep?*

He needed a plan. Sneaking around had been kind of helpful, and he'd learned some good things about Tacita and the pirates' plans, but if he was actually going to stop them, he needed to go further. He needed to fight back, actively and aggressively. He'd learned in the computer room that there was no way he could take on the whole group at once, so he'd have to split them up. But how?

The first one he needed to take care of was Kratt. He wasn't the smartest pirate on the ship, but he was definitely the most dangerous. So, what could Zero do to incapacitate Kratt? Tie him up? Maybe, but how could he get him to hold still long enough to tie him? Wait for him to sleep? He didn't have enough time for that. Maybe he could force him to sleep. There might be some sedatives in the medical cargo somewhere, but even if Zero could find it there was no way he'd be able to get close enough to stick Kratt with it. He needed another plan.

Zero tried to remember what his dad had always taught him: try to break down a problem into pieces, and solve them one by one. So the first problem was: how could he get Kratt alone somewhere? He needed bait, and he needed bait that only Kratt would follow. That meant it couldn't be subtle—and it had to be dangerous. Kratt was the bruiser, the one everyone else would send into trouble instead of risking themselves. So, what was dangerous enough that the others wouldn't follow him?

Zero winced when he realized the answer: the outside of the ship. They had a mining suit back on the Drago—the one with all the hooks and loops on it. If Zero got back in his own space suit and went outside, and then did something flashy to get their attention, they'd put Kratt in the mining suit and send him out to deal with it. Especially if Zero was doing something harmful, like attacking their ship. Kratt would come out in a fury, and then all Zero would have to do was ... what? Trap him outside? That wouldn't work—there were way too many airlocks to get him back inside, and the rest of the pirates would help.

But if he trapped him *to* something ...

The communicators crackled to life. "I don't see him anywhere," said Jim.

"I told you he wasn't an alien," said Nyx.

"Spider," said Mama, "any luck on Ring 280?"

"No," Spider snapped, "and I shouldn't be out here anyway. I've got a flight path to calculate!"

"You've got twelve hours," said Mama.

"Ten," said Jim.

Only ten hours left? thought Zero. His stomach grumbled. He hadn't eaten or slept in ages.

"I can smell him," growled Kratt.

"No you can't," said Nyx.

"Shut up, brat."

"Kratt!" yelled Mama. "Don't you sass her, you hear?

She's the one that saw this boy while the rest of you were banging your heads into walls like a bunch of squawking chickens."

"Sorry, Mama."

"No other ships have docked with us," said Jim, "so he has to be one of the colonists."

"One of the kids," said Nyx. "He was small."

I'm not that *small,* thought Zero.

"Spider," sighed Mama, "come on back up and program your flight plan. Kratt and Jim can keep looking, and one kid isn't a big threat anyway."

"Thanks," said Spider.

"I'm going to find him and kill him," snarled Kratt. "I'm going to skin him alive!"

"Why did we bring the psycho?" asked Jim.

"He's my boy," said Mama. "Now: stop complaining, and find that kid!"

I have to find a way to stop Kratt, thought Zero. *What do I know about him? He's violent, and he's scary, but mostly he's just angry. He jumps into things without thinking.*

And that gives me a plan ...

Zero made a list of the things he'd need—a chain, a space suit, a second space suit, and some of those self-sealing bolts. Oh! And he'd need paint. Not the liquid stuff he'd used on his brothers; he needed spray paint. He'd seen some in that same cargo bay, closed tight in a stasis crate. Zero felt bad about opening another crate, but figured the colonists would understand.

"I'm sorry you're missing some spray paint," he whispered, pretending he was talking to the colonists. "On the other hand, you're not a slave in a mine on a secret evil pirate planet, so I think you can deal with it."

The communicator crackled again: "I'm going to search Section A," said Jim. "You take E."

"Fine," grumbled Kratt.

"That means Section C is open for a few minutes," whispered Zero, and slipped out of his hiding place.

Time to fight some pirates.

CHAPTER 20
PLAN B

ZERO STOOD IN THE AIRLOCK AGAIN, THE BAGGY SPACE SUIT floating around him. He'd used a rope for a belt this time, cinching it tight so he could see and maneuver a little better. The outer pockets were filled with supplies: self-sealing bolts, a length of heavy chain, and two cans of spray paint—just in case. Tucked under his left arm was a second space suit, and under his right was a hammer.

He took a breath, checked his seals again, and opened the airlock door.

The empty hangar yawned open in front of him, and he walked across it slowly in his heavy magnetic boots. He reached the wall and thought about jumping up and out of the hangar, but that vast, empty nothingness above him freaked him out, so instead he just put his feet on the wall—first one boot, then the next—and walked straight up the side. It made him uncomfortable at first, but then he remembered what his mother had said—there was no true down in space, so why not make it whatever he wanted it to be? He started to think of the wall as the floor, and suddenly it was

—he felt as if the whole ship had stood on its side suddenly, just to match his new orientation. He reached the top of the wall and stepped out onto the outer hull of the Pathfinder and reoriented himself again. If he always thought of his feet as down and his head as up, it made the walk much easier.

Which was good, because he had half a skyscraper to walk up the side of.

The hangar was on Ring 42, and the Drago was docked on 240. That was more than half a kilometer away, which would have been easy on Earth but was slow and exhausting in the magnetic boots. Every now and then the communicator crackled, with Jim or Kratt reporting that they still hadn't found anybody, and Mama demanding that they try harder. When he finally reached the Drago, he stopped and took stock of it. Having already been inside of it, he found the outside less menacing than he'd expected—no skull and crossbones or anything like that, just a squat, boxy ship with a couple of round pods on the sides. It looked like it had landed on its belly, sitting on the Pathfinder like a toad on a log. Zero studied the ship as he approached, looking for the most important part of his plan: the Drago had its own outer airlock, on the side by one of the bedrooms. And that was almost certainly where Kratt would come out.

Zero needed to get on top of the Drago, but the docking tube connecting the two ships was mostly plastic and rubber. So he couldn't do his "walk up the wall" trick this time. He'd have to jump. The thought of it made him queasy —he'd be close to both ships, but he wouldn't be touching either of them. He'd be alone in outer space, billions of kilometers from even an asteroid, floating free and untethered. Even if it was only for a second, it scared him to death.

He put the hammer through his belt, made sure his glove was as firmly in place as he could get it, and looked up at the Drago above him. It had handholds here and there, or things that could be used as handholds. He picked one, focused on it, and turned off the magnets in his boots.

He jumped.

It felt like an eternity, hanging in space, drifting out and away from the Pathfinder, but it was really only a meter. Then the Drago came in reach, and he grabbed at the handhold on the side of it, clinging to it with all his strength. He gripped it tightly, brought his legs around, and reactivated the magnets. They clamped onto the hull of the Drago, and Zero stood up. He changed his perspective as he walked, moving around the outside the ship until he was standing on the top. He held up the extra space suit and positioned it carefully, facing away from the Drago's airlock. When he was certain it was in the right place, he let go of it; with no gravity or air currents to move it, the suit simply floated there, motionless, just like someone was standing in it.

Everything seemed so still and silent, Zero had to remind himself that they were currently traveling at four million kilometers an hour. But the motion was relative, like his father had said—he and the Drago and the empty space suit and everything else were also traveling at four million kilometers an hour, so without any air to provide resistance, there was nothing to slow them down. They may as well have been standing still.

"Okay," said Zero. "Now let's get some pirates' attention." He walked across the ship, looking for a target sensitive enough to raise an alarm. He found a sensor panel and walked toward it. "May as well start here." He pulled the hammer from his belt, held it firmly, and banged on the sensor panel until it cracked.

It took a few seconds—long, agonizing seconds—but finally the communicator buzzed to life.

"Hey guys," said Spider, "I just got an alert from the Drago's computer. Looks like one of the sensors failed?"

"We can fix it later," said Mama. "Keep working."

"Oh, come on," said Zero. He sighed, looked for another target, and found it—an antenna. This one he didn't even bother to hit; he just grabbed it in his hands and snapped it in half.

"Weird," said Spider. "I just got another alert. We lost an antenna."

"It's probably just a computer failure," said Jim. "If the internal diagnostic system broke, it would start sending us all kinds of false alarms."

Mama snarled. "You told me you fixed that system, Spider."

"I did," said Spider. "It was working perfectly."

"Well things don't just break for no reason," said Mama.

"That's what I'm saying," said Spider. "We need to at least look and see which system is broken."

Zero found another external sensor node, and smashed it to pieces.

"We lost a camera," said Spider. "This is definitely not normal. Somebody go see what's going on!"

"Fine," said Mama. "I'm closest, so I'll go look. But if it's just that diagnostic system and you didn't fix it right, I'm going to be hopping mad."

Zero smashed a few more things, then walked over to the Drago's cockpit, waiting just out of view of the window. A few minutes later, Mama spoke over the communicator again.

"I'm here," she said. "Where's that diagnostic terminal, girl? You left this place in such a mess."

Zero didn't wait any longer. He raised the hammer, stood up, and walked right in front of the cockpit window.

Mama was muttering. "Can't find a thing in this—aaahh-hhh!" She saw Zero and jumped back, waving her arms in terror. Zero waved, raised his hammer, and slammed it down on the window—there was no way he could break the special glass, but it looked super menacing, and Mama yelped again. "It's that boy!" she shrieked. "He's here, on the outside of the ship!" Zero banged on the glass again, and she shouted rage into the communicator. "He's breaking everything! Somebody, get out there and stop him!"

"I'll tear him apart!" shouted Kratt.

Zero looked at Mama, waggled his hammer, and walked out of view.

"He's moved onto the top of the ship!" Mama screamed. "Get him now!"

Zero moved quickly. He walked to the empty floating space suit, threw the hammer away, and pulled out his next group of tools: a chain in one hand and a self-sealing bolt in another. He walked about two meters toward the back of the ship, and used the bolt to weld one end of the chain to a handhold on the hull. All he had to do was wrap the chain through the handle, sliding a bolt through the links, and hit the button. The bolt didn't spark like before, because outside of the ship there was no oxygen to burn. But it glowed white-hot and welded itself and the chain to the hull of the Drago.

"He's getting away!" shouted Mama. "Hurry!"

Kratt roared back, incoherent and furious. Zero kept his calm, and dragged the free end of the chain to his hiding place: the flared end of a rocket thruster on the back of the ship. It was just big enough to hold him and keep him hidden from view. As long as Kratt didn't notice the chain—and Zero was desperately hoping that the big floating space suit would grab all of Kratt's attention—he would never see Zero at all.

Zero felt a faint hum through his feet. The Drago's outer airlock sliding open.

Kratt's voice rumbled in Zero's ears. "I'm outside."

"He's up on top," said Mama.

Kratt started walking, and Zero held his breath.

"I see him," said Kratt, and laughed maliciously. Zero counted to five, waiting for the pirate to walk past his hiding place, and then turned off his magnetic boots and floated out into space. He held the edge of the thruster, watching Kratt charge across the hull and tackle the empty space suit. The pirate thrashed around, literally trying to tear the suit apart, while Zero pushed himself off of the thruster and floated up behind him, silent as a ghost. Kratt slowed, and then stopped.

"There's nobody in this suit," said Kratt.

Zero slipped the chain through one of the metal loops on the back of Kratt's suit, stuck a self-sealing bolt through the middle of it, and hit the button.

"What's that?" shouted Kratt, and spun around. Zero saw him face-to-face, barely half a meter away, Kratt's face twisted in fury. The pirate lunged to grab him, and Zero tried desperately to get away, pushing himself backward, fumbling in his pocket for a can of spray paint. Kratt almost grabbed him, but Zero dodged. Kratt swung his hand again, glove curled like a claw, and then Zero had the paint can— he pointed it at Kratt's face, hit the button, and sprayed. The paint that came out froze almost instantly, hitting Kratt's faceplate in sticky crystals instead of an even layer, but that didn't matter. Zero wasn't using the paint as paint, he was using it as propulsion. The force of the spray can wouldn't have moved him a millimeter on Earth, but here in zero gravity it pushed him backward, just out of reach of Kratt's hands. Kratt kept coming, and Zero kept spraying and then Kratt stopped, yanked back by the chain.

"That's the end of your leash, buddy," said Zero. Kratt stopped, braced himself, and surged forward again. But again the chain yanked him back. Zero waved at the furious pirate, laughing as Kratt struggled, but in doing so, Zero's gloves slipped, and he dropped the can.

Zero was about three meters away from the Drago, and floating slowly farther every second.

Off into space.

"Ha!" roared Kratt over the intercom. "I got him."

"Good!" said Mama. "Bring him in."

"That's … not what I meant," said Kratt.

"So you don't have him?" asked Nyx.

"Not in my hands," said Kratt, "but I chased him away. He's floating off into space, without a ship or a jetpack or a tether. We'll never see him again."

"Ha!" said Mama. "That will show him."

Zero reached into his other pocket, and pulled out his second can of spray paint.

"Just in case," he said, and turned around, and used the sprayer to propel himself down to the surface of the

Pathfinder. His boots hit the hull, and he activated the magnets.

"No!" shouted Kratt.

"What happened?" asked Mama.

"He got back to the ship!"

"Then go get him," said Mama, "and do it right this time!"

Kratt tugged on his chain.

"I can't move," Kratt roared. "He chained me to the hull!"

"What?" asked Jim.

"You idiot!" screamed Mama.

"I think I like this kid," said Spider.

Zero waved at Kratt and turned to walk away, moving around the curve of the ship and out of sight. He didn't want anyone to see which airlock he used to get back inside.

"Come out and get me!" shouted Kratt.

"How? That's our only space suit!" said Jim.

"There's got to be more somewhere," said Kratt. "Find one!"

"If we have time," said Mama. "Right now we've got bigger things to worry about than helping an idiot."

"You can't leave me out here, Mama!"

"Your rebreather's got plenty of air," said Mama. "You'll be fine till we can get to you. For now: Spider, Jim, *find that boy!*"

CHAPTER 21

TOMATO SAUCE

ZERO RACED BACK TO THE EMPTY HANGAR, THREW HIMSELF into the airlock, and hit the button. The tiny room pressurized, filling with air, and when the light turned green Zero pulled off his helmet and gasped. It was the same air he had in his suit, but there was more of it. He'd felt like he was suffocating in that thing.

The communicator crackled: "Someone just used an airlock on Ring 42," said Spider. "It's one of the landing barge hangars."

"Got it," said Jim.

"Crap!" said Zero. They'd been watching the airlocks on the ship's computer! He had to get away from here as fast as he could. He opened the inner door, stripped off the rest of the space suit, and pulled it with him toward the cargo bay to hide it. After a few meters he saw a streak of blue out of the corner of his eye, on the sleeve of the white space suit, and realized there was paint on the fingers—sticky globs left over from the spray cans. Zero looked behind himself in a panic and saw a small spot on the wall, and then another, and then another; he'd left a tiny trail of bright blue paint smears all the way here from the airlock! He let go of the space suit immediately, knowing that it was safer to just leave it here and get as far away as possible. He pushed off the wall, flew a fewer meters down the passage, then stopped in another panic and launched himself back toward the suit: if he left them another space suit, they could go outside and get Kratt. The rebreather was removable, so he pulled it out, leaving the suit useless, then raced down the hall as fast as he could go. He didn't know if he had time to make it all the way to his hideout in the construction supplies, so he raced instead to the cargo bay full of food. He reached it in record time, fled inside, and closed the door behind him. He squeezed back into the gaps between the crates, and waited. His heart pounded in his chest.

"I'm here." Jim's voice rang loud in Zero's ears, and he yelped and flinched before remembering that it was just the communicator.

Don't find me. Don't find me, Zero thought.

"There's some paint smears on the walls, so I might be able to follow him—aw, wait, here's the space suit. Looks like he left it in the middle of a hall."

Zero shook his head in relief. He was so glad he'd seen the paint before it was too late.

"Where did he go from there?" asked Mama.

"I can't tell," said Jim. "No, wait—there's some more paint."

Zero's heart froze. *More paint?* Zero looked at himself frantically, trying to find some paint he had missed, and found a small smear of it on his hip. He'd been so scared in the hallway, he hadn't thought to check himself, only the space suit. He squeezed further back into the maze of crates, praying that he hadn't left any smears that could lead them to the cargo bay.

"Found some more," said Jim's voice. "And some more. And—no, that's it. The trail stops here."

"Where?" asked Mama.

"A few meters away from one of the cargo bays," said Jim. "Maybe he's hiding inside."

The door to Zero's cargo bay slid open with a soft swoosh. Light flooded in. Zero held his breath, though he was so far back behind the crates that there was no way Jim would see him.

But he might see more paint ...

Zero's heart pounded in his chest. He heard Jim's breathing, and then a sharp tap on one of the crates. Sweat beaded on Zero's skin, and then instead of dripping to the floor it floated off of him, hanging in the air around him like a rainfall frozen in time. Zero counted the seconds: one, two, three, four, five. What was Jim seeing? What would he do? Thirteen, fourteen, fifteen, sixteen, seventeen. The breathing moved closer. Another loud knock.

"He didn't come in here," said Jim. Zero heard his voice twice—once in person, and again a second later in the earphones from the communicator.

"You sure?" asked Mama.

"There's no paint inside the cargo bay," said Jim. "Plus, these crates are stacked so close together there's nowhere for him to go. I'll check the bay across the hall." He left, and the door closed behind him.

Zero didn't dare to breathe again for several seconds. He

was safe—for now. And part one of his plan had worked: Kratt was stranded outside, with no way to get back in. Better yet, he was chained to the Drago, so when the pirates flew away they'd take him with them. *But that's the whole problem,* thought Zero. *How do I get the pirates to fly away?*

Zero's stomach growled, so loudly he worried that Jim might hear it through the wall. He squeezed his way through the maze of crates until he found the open one, and reached in to find food. He probed around with his hand, found another box of banana chips, and pulled it out. He peeled it open and ate ravenously, but as his hunger lessened his thirst got worse and worse. He rooted around in the crate for something to drink, but all he could find that had liquid in it was another can of tomato sauce. He stared at the label, grimacing, and finally popped it open and took a long gulp. It was thick, but it was liquid, and it helped calm his thirst for now. "Good thing you're not infected like that other can," he whispered. "If I'd taken a drink of that stuff, hoo boy—"

And then he stopped, and a slow grin spread across his face.

"They've got crowbars and stun guns," he said, "but I've got tomato sauce."

Zero left the can of good tomato sauce floating in the air, and looked behind him for the bad one. Where had he stashed it? Aha! There it was. He pulled it out of a gap between two crates, feeling the bulge in the sides and the lid. Anyone who ate even a drop of this stuff would get so sick they wouldn't be able to leave the toilet for a week. They'd be trapped almost as securely as Kratt was. If Zero could get it into their food ... but how?

He couldn't just walk up and put it on food they'd

already prepared, because there was no way to get in and out unseen. But if he could get to the meal packs before they ate them, he could just add a drop or two to all of them—no matter which one they ate, they'd get too sick to move. But he had to be fast, and he had to be agile, and that meant he couldn't haul the entire bulging can of tomato sauce with him. He needed something he could use to carry a smaller dose. He hunted around in the opened food crate to see what he could find: Shrink-wrapped pickles. Cream of Mushroom soup. Protein powder. Instant coffee with filters and stirring straws. Maybe the filters would work? No: the straws. He dipped one into the good tomato sauce, just as a test, and pulled it out. The sauce was thick enough that it stayed in the straw, and the lack of gravity meant it didn't drip out. He used a shrink-wrapped pickle to wipe off the excess sauce, and ta-da! He had a perfect dose of weaponized food poisoning—just stab it into the meal brick and let the pooping commence.

He grabbed the straws and the bulging can, and moved to a different part of the cargo bay. He didn't want to risk contaminating the food he actually ate. He peeled open the can—it smelled bad, but not so strong it would tip them off —and prepared a few straws full of spoiled sauce. He didn't have pockets in this Pathfinder coverall, but he had a little belt around his waist; he tucked the straws into that, and worked his way back to the door.

Jim was still searching the cargo bays, calling out his position to Mama every now and then, so Zero knew exactly where he was. And Spider was presumably still up in the control room, programming a new flight path to Tacita, so Zero knew where she was, too. It was Mama he couldn't predict—and Nyx. He didn't dare to forget Nyx again. Where were those two? What were they doing? Wherever they were, they were probably together, because they weren't talking over the communicator. Zero opened the door, slipped into the hall, and closed it behind him.

CHAPTER 22
PLAN C

"Ring 56, Section C," said Jim. "It's a cargo bay full of solar panels. No kid."

"I can't believe you can't find a kid," said Mama. "He's just a child! You're supposed to be smarter than a child, Jim."

Zero moved through a narrow aisle of stasis pods on Ring 52, toward the maintenance tube in Section B. As soon as Jim announced his next target—a cargo bay on Ring 56, Section H—Zero slipped into the B tube and jumped up, traveling several Rings and shooting right past 56 in a flash. With Jim far behind him he breathed a little easier, but he was still spooked by Mama and Nyx. Where were they?

Zero changed tubes frequently, trying to make himself as unpredictable as possible. He didn't want to stay in one place, or on one path, any longer than necessary. It kept him hidden, but it slowed him down, and it took him almost an hour to reach Ring 240. If he was going to ruin their food, he had to make sure he got *all* their food, and that meant the meal bricks in the Drago as well as the Pathfinder. He hovered out of sight near the Drago's

entrance, listening, but it didn't sound like anyone was
there. He pulled himself closer, certain that there would be
a guard—maybe Nyx—since she didn't seem to be
anywhere else. But he heard nothing. He peeked out, and
saw an empty hallway. Four pirates were not enough to
keep watch over an entire spaceship. He took the risk and
jumped across the open space, through the door, and into
the Drago. It was mostly as he'd left it, though if possible it
was even messier—when Kratt had taken the space suit,
he'd apparently scattered everything else that cargo net had
been holding all over of the main room. It occurred to Zero
that Kratt might be looking in from outside, so he stayed
away from the cockpit windows just in case. He maneu-
vered through the floating clutter and hunted for the
pirates' food stores. Every few seconds he looked back at
the entrance, expecting to see one of the pirates walking in
on him with a stun gun. He searched in the cargo nets, he
searched in the lockers, he even searched in the disgusting
bathroom again. Finally he found a large cooler shoved
under one of the sleeping bag wall-beds, but when he
opened it he found only a handful of ration packs—six
small meal bricks, all of them labeled "Chicken Stroganoff."
Apparently none of the pirates liked chicken stroganoff. He
jumped back to the bedroom door, looking across to the
main ship entrance, but saw no one.

Time to do this, Zero thought.

He flew back to the cooler, unwrapped a corner of each
meal, and used one of his tomato sauce straws to dab a bit of
spoiled food into each one. He closed them up again,
stashed the empty straw in one of the sleeping bags, and fled
back out of the Drago. He'd done it! But he wasn't sure it

would do him any good: no one was likely to eat those meal bricks anytime soon.

He had to go up to the fore of the ship—to the rec room and the rest of the food. He slipped out of the Drago and back into the Pathfinder.

"I'm sick of searching," said Jim on the communicator. "I'm coming back up."

"No, that's where I'm going!" whispered Zero.

"You stay until you find him," said Mama.

"Yes, what she said," said Zero to himself.

"This ship is a kilometer long and a hundred meters wide," said Jim. His voice was angry now. "That's almost eight million cubic meters of volume, and that kid probably takes up half a cubic meter at best. I'm not going to find him until he does something stupid, and I'm hungry and tired, so I'm coming back up!"

Zero grimaced. "No!"

"Check the Drago, then," said Mama, and Zero froze in the hallway, mouth open.

"No way," said Zero. "Am I really that lucky?"

"Nyx was supposed to be watching it, but I haven't heard from her in a while."

"You think he got her?" asked Jim.

"I think she's off screwing around, like usual," said Mama.

"Fine," said Jim, "I'll check the ship."

Zero punched the air in excitement—his plan was going to work! But then he realized he was floating in plain view, right where Jim was headed, and pushed himself into the nearest aisle of stasis pods to hide. Should he wait? Or just head up to the control room now? Better to keep moving. He floated all the way around to the opposite side of the ship, and then peeked into a maintenance tube. No Jim in this one, and no one in the other direction, either. He pulled himself in and jumped up, moving as quickly as he could. When he reached Ring 299 he heard voices: Mama and Spider were arguing.

"... then it doesn't matter," said Mama, "because we'll catch him eventually anyway."

"One of him, maybe," said Spider. "Twenty thousand of him? You go on and on about having twenty thousand workers in your mine, but this one kids shows exactly why that's a bad idea. How are you going to keep control of that many people?"

"Once we're on Tacita, we can use guns again," said Mama. "That'll keep 'em in line."

Spider answered around a mouthful of food: "We're a tiny outpost. We have a thousand bullets, at best. That's nineteen thousand colonists left to overrun us."

Zero inched closer. Both women were in the rec room, and by the sounds of it they were eating. He was too late! He wanted to float over toward the door, so he could peek in, but that would mean going out into the central column. What if Jim saw him? And where was Nyx?

He hesitated, and then doubled back toward the maintenance tubes. He could hide in the last place they'd ever expect to see him again: in the computer banks. He found the same hatch he'd used before, and slipped inside.

"I'm back at the Drago," said Jim. "Everything's fine. I'm coming up—"

"You wanted to eat," said Mama, "so eat in the Drago.

Someone's got to eat those chicken stroganoffs, and you're the one that bought 'em."

Zero did a little antigravity dance of joy.

"They were cheap!" said Jim.

"Just eat one," said Spider.

"And watch the Drago," said Mama. "Sooner or later that kid's going to think about going in there, and then we're all in trouble."

That made Zero pause. What was in the Drago that could put them all in trouble? Or was she just being dramatic about the invasion of their personal space?

Either way, Jim was about to eat a spoiled meal, and that'd be one more pirate down—

"Uh oh," said Jim. "Green Alert."

Zero floated closer to the rec room wall, and heard Spider's confused response through the vent: "What's a green alert?"

Mama sighed. "That's when he thinks there's an alien." She got on the communicator. "For crying out loud, Jim, there's no alien!"

"Something's gotten into the meal bricks!" said Jim. "Not a person—it's a creature. Something was nibbling on the corners!"

"Maybe it's a rat," said Spider.

"We don't have rats," said Mama. "Kratt ate them all."

"Something was poking into these meal bricks with … hollow teeth! What has hollow teeth? I swear to you. It's an alien!" Jim insisted.

Zero looked at his little coffee straws. They did kind of look like long, hollow teeth.

"Stop making up stories!" said Spider. "You just don't want to eat the stroganoff!"

Zero could see the women clearly now through the vent: Spider and Mama, floating in the rec room with their meals in front of them. Some kind of burrito thing? They both had one, whatever it was, and they were both ignoring their food, talking on the communicators instead. It would have been the perfect opportunity to poke the food with some spoiled tomato sauce, but they were too far away. Maybe if Kratt had actually managed to rip the vent off the wall, Zero could reach his arm through and stab the lasagna, but even that might be too far away. What could he do?

"I'm not going to eat this," said Jim. "It's contaminated." Zero scowled. *He was so close!*

"Suit yourself," said Mama, "but stay in that ship. I don't want that kid to start snooping around."

"I'm throwing this away," said Jim, and Mama turned away from her food in a rage, pushing herself toward the door.

"Just because you don't want it doesn't mean nobody else will!"

Now Spider was the only one looking at the burritos.

"It's contaminated!" shouted Jim. "It's not safe."

"I'm done here," said Spider. "You two argue all you want —I'm going back to the control room." She pushed past Mama, and suddenly no one was looking at the food. It was right there, in front of Zero, unattended but out of reach. He looked at the straw in his hand; it would easily fit through the slats in the vent. Maybe he could throw it? Or—

The answer was so simple he almost laughed. With the sauce in the straw it was basically a blow dart. He slid one end through the vent, aimed it carefully, took a big breath, then put his mouth on the clean end of the straw and blew. A tiny blob of tomato sauce flew out, crossed the room, and splatted on the wall behind the burrito.

He missed!

He took another straw, aimed carefully, and blew. He hit the chair.

He had one tomato straw left. Mama couldn't keep yelling at Jim for too much longer. He poked the straw through the vent, aimed, and blew.

The bacteria-ridden tomato sauce sailed across the room in a perfect, straight line, and splashed onto one of the burritos. But whose? Mama turned around, and Zero pulled the straw back through the vent and out of view.

Mama floated back to the burritos, grabbed the contaminated one, and took a bite. She frowned as she ate the tiny blob of tomato sauce. "This salsa's really bland."

Zero silently punched the air in triumph.

CHAPTER 23

CAUGHT

Zero was out of the spoiled food, and he'd only gotten one person. Should he go back for more? Could he come up with another plan? Mama was obviously the boss, so stranding her in a bathroom was pretty good, but Jim and Spider and Nyx were all still on the loose, and they were more likely to catch him than she was anyway. Mama was mostly just coordinating things from a central location, through the communicators, and she could still do that even if the location was a bathroom.

He considered, just for a second, trying to reboot Sancho right now, but decided not to risk it. Spider would just turn him off again, and this time, she might do it in a way that Zero couldn't fix. Better to keep going and hope he could get rid of the pirates. He needed more sauce. Getting them sick might take a while, but it was still his best plan.

He slipped out through the hatch and headed aft, going slow and watching out for Jim. When he finally made it back to the cargo bay he crept inside, closed the door, and breathed a sigh of relief.

"Boo," said a voice, and Zero yelped in fright. He looked around wildly, pushing himself toward the door, but Nyx was right there, blocking it with her body. Zero backed up, yelping again, and then braced himself to attack. If he could take her out now, while she was alone, he could—

"Nope," said Nyx, and raised her stun gun, pointing it straight at his chest. "You just stay right there, and we can have a little talk." Now that he got a closer look at her, he decided he was right about her age—twelve, maybe even thirteen. She had bright pink hair that billowed around her like a jellyfish, and a devious smirk that showed she meant business.

"Don't kill me," said Zero.

"It's just a stun gun, you big baby, it can't kill you."

"But Kratt will," he said. "Or Mama."

"How do you know our names? Ohhhh." She nodded her head, as if everything made sense. "You're wearing head-phones. Do you have one of our communicators?"

Zero clenched his jaw, wondering how he could possibly get out of this.

"I guess that explains how you've been able to hide from us," said Nyx. "Jim keeps calling out his location like some kind of military genius, and you're just listening in and laughing your head off."

Zero didn't know what to say. "Well I haven't been ... laughing, really."

"Give it to me," said Nyx. Zero didn't move.

"Come on," said Nyx, waving the stun gun. "Give me the communicator—and the headphones." Zero grimaced and pulled it out of his pocket, tossing both the device and the headphones toward her. They drifted lazily through the air, and she caught them with her free hand. She looked at them in surprise. "No way," she said, examining them. "This is one of ours, isn't it? These are Spider's headphones." She looked at Zero and raised her eyebrow. "You went into our ship— you looted our ship." She smiled. "Not bad."

"It seemed fair," said Zero, finding his courage again. "You're trying to steal mine."

"Oh, so it's *your* ship?" asked Nyx. "Well pardon me, Governor Tamira Hatendi of the Kaguya Colony Pathfinder mission. I didn't recognize you without your United Earth uniform." She stared at him for a moment, thinking. Then she asked another question. "What'd you do to Big Mama?"

"What?"

"You said Kratt and Mama would kill you," said Nyx. "Kratt, obviously, I know why he'd kill you, but why Big Mama? What'd you do to her?"

"Nothing."

She cocked her head to the side, considering him. "What's your name?"

"What are you going to do to me?"

"I'm going to ask you your name," said Nyx, "over and over again, until you tell me."

"I'm ... Zero," said Zero.

"There's no way that's your real name."

"Is Nyx your real name?"

"Okay then," said Nyx, smiling again but keeping the stun gun trained on his chest. "Nicknames it is. Are you really alone?"

Zero shook his head. "There's a whole team of United Earth commandos hiding in one of the cargo bays."

"They're super bad at their jobs," said Nyx.

"Fine, I'm alone," admitted Zero. "But you gotta admit, I'm doing a pretty good job for one lone kid."

"You are doing a fantastic job," Nyx agreed. "You chained Kratt to the outside of a spaceship! Honestly, that deserves an award."

"So let me go."

"No backsies," said Nyx. "I got you fair and square."

"How'd you know I was coming here?" asked Zero. "Jim said I wasn't in this bay."

"He said the spaces here were too small to move through," said Nyx. "Which, of course, made me wonder how big they really were, because Jim is not a small guy. I came down here, realized I could fit through these little gaps in the crates pretty easy, and then I found your open food crate and I knew for sure."

"It was open when I found it," said Zero.

"Aliens?" asked Nyx.

"Probably."

"Your aliens really like tomato sauce," said Nyx. "You've got two open cans of it back there."

"Did you eat any?"

She frowned. "Did I eat any of the random open cans of tomato sauce I found floating in a cargo hold?"

"You don't have to be rude about it."

"But I choose to be." Nyx looked at him for a moment, then shrugged. "So, now what do I do with you?"

Zero smiled. "Let me go?"

"You'd make a terrible pirate," said Nyx.

"Tell that to Kratt."

Nyx nodded. "See, Kratt is the problem: if I take you back to the family, Kratt will, as you said, kill you. And I don't want you to die—you're on the other team, but you're still pretty cool. And there's nobody cool on Tacita."

"Are you really from Tacita?" asked Zero. "Like an honest-to-goodness hidden planet on the edge of the solar system?"

"You better believe it," said Nyx.

"What's it like?"

Nyx paused, as if the question surprised her, then shrugged again. "Awful. It's cold and it's dark. We're so far away from the sun that it just looks like another star. Like we have no sun at all. The atmosphere keeps us from literally freezing, but we can't breathe it, so we live in old ships and in holes in the ground."

"That sucks."

"It really does."

"How'd you get there?" Zero asked.

"Me? I was born there. Everyone else found it by accident in a failed mining expedition about fifteen years ago. A couple thousand people. It took them five years to get the ships repaired. And in the meanwhile, they did what they do best and started mining. Turns out, there's enough molybdenum out there to supply the whole solar system for a thousand years."

"What's molybdenum?"

"I don't have the faintest idea."

Zero stared, and then laughed. And after a moment, Nyx laughed with him. Small chuckles giving way to loud guffaws. Both of them laughing and laughing until they could barely breathe. "Oh man! You don't have the faintest idea, and neither do I."

"It's some kind of metal, I think. And they're ready to

burn down the whole friggin' system for it. And I have zero clue what it is or what it's for or anything. Adults are the worst."

Zero thought about his parents. "Some adults are okay."

"None of the ones I know. I mean, you've seen my mother. You want to guess where my father is?"

"You mean Jim?"

"He's my step-grandfather, actually. He joined us about six years ago when we started selling molybdenum back to the inner planets. Most of the Tacita miners are content being secret traders, but Big Mama wants more. She found out that Jim was the Pathfinder pilot and hatched this whole scheme to use him as an inside man."

"So, who's your dad, then?"

Nyx settled into her story, visibly pleased to have someone new she could talk to. "It doesn't matter who, just where—and that's dead. He was killed in the first Tacita mutiny. See, Big Mama didn't used to be in charge, so she tried to take over and used her own sons as muscle. Got my daddy killed a month or two before I was even born. And if she ever feels sorry about it, she's pretty good at hiding it. Throws it in Spider's face sometimes. Or in Kratt's—making it out like it's their fault. She's the one that ran the whole thing, though."

"So your mom is Spider?"

"Not that you can tell by watching her. She treats me like garbage, and just lets Big Mama raise me. And I guess my father would have been about the same. All I know about him is that he fell in love with Spider, and anyone who'd do that is crazy. So I figure I'm better off not knowing him."

"Wow," said Zero. "I'm sorry." It was starting to make

sense to him why Nyx was so eager to talk. She didn't have anyone in her family—maybe her whole life—that she could trust or feel comfortable with.

"And the worst part is ..." Nyx paused, like she was listening to something. She waited, then gave Zero a wary glance. "See? Case in point."

"What happened?"

"Oh—I forgot you lost your communicator," said Nyx, and tapped her ears, revealing wireless headphones. "Big Mama just told me to come back where it's safe, and my darling mother said I could fend for myself, and good riddance if I couldn't."

"That sucks," said Zero, thinking of his own mother. He looked back up. "Though to be fair, you're the only one who caught me, right? So you can fend for yourself."

"Well, that's not really the part that bothers me, is it?"

"Can I ask you a question?" asked Zero.

"I might not answer," said Nyx, "but you can ask me anything you want."

"Are you really going to enslave us all? Like, all twenty thousand people?"

Nyx looked away, like she felt embarrassed, or even guilty. "That's ... not what this is."

"I heard Mama say it," said Zero. "You're going to make us work in a mine."

"Well, I didn't know that when we started."

"But you know it now. Are you just going to let them?"

"Maybe that's none of your business." She raised the stun gun again. "I don't have to explain this stuff to you."

"Sorry," said Zero again. Apparently he'd struck a nerve. "I just ... I like having someone to talk to."

Nyx stared at him for a while before answering. "Yeah," she said at last.

He stared back, waiting for her to stun him or call for Jim, or any number of other scenarios—all bad for him. But she didn't do anything. Finally he dared to speak. "So ..." She didn't shoot him, so he tried again. "What are you going to do now?"

"I don't know." She twisted her face into a couple of weird expressions, trying to think. "Will you stop attacking us?"

"So you can enslave me?"

"I can make sure you're okay," she said.

"Do you mean 'living an exciting new life on a bright new planet' okay, or just 'slightly better off than the rest of the slaves in a deep space mine' okay?"

Nyx threw up her hands. "Well, what do you want me to do? Betray my family?"

"Your family is evil."

She shoved the gun closer to his face. "Say that again."

"I mean—" He stopped, searching for something to say. "Come with us. To Kaguya."

"There's not enough stasis pods," said Nyx. "I looked."

"If you looked, it's because you want to come," said Zero. "Tacita's terrible—you said so yourself. Kaguya's awesome. There's got to be something we could—" She stopped him before he could continue, holding up one hand while she put her other to her ear. She listened for a moment, then pointed the stun gun at him again.

"What did you do to Big Mama?"

"Nothing," said Zero, "I told you."

"Did you poison her?" asked Nyx. "She says she feels like

she's dying—vomiting, diarrhea." Nyx looked genuinely worried. "She's the only one who's nice to me."

"She'll be fine," said Zero, starting to feel bad and trying to reassure her. "I just made her a little sick, but she'll get better, and—" He didn't get to finish his sentence, because Nyx shot him with the stun gun: the nose of the weapon blew open, and two metal darts flew out, trailing wires behind them. They hit him, and the electrical current surged through his body, and he blacked out.

CHAPTER 24

PAPER, ROCK, AND SCISSORS

ZERO WOKE UP IN THE DARK, FLOATING IN THE CARGO BAY. HIS head hurt, and his chest ached where the stun gun darts had hit him. But he was alive, and he was healthy.

And he was alone.

There was no sign of Nyx, or of where she might have gone. Zero assumed she'd gone back to find Big Mama, which meant she was probably going to tell the others where he was. But why had she just left him? Why not take him with her? It's not like it was hard to carry someone around in zero gravity—she could just shove him along in front of her, all the way up the central column of the ship. She didn't want him to screw up their plans, but she didn't want him to die, either. Maybe her solution was just to ... leave him?

There was no way he was going to give up. With Mama sick and Kratt still outside, they were down to just three pirates, and one of them was a little girl, and she'd already used her stun gun. Those things only had one shot each. He opened the door and checked the nearest computer panel, showing him the countdown. It was almost time to cross the

Kuiper Cliff. He'd been unconscious for hours. He didn't have much time, but he still had some, and he was going to use it. All or nothing. Do or die.

He didn't like that last thought, but he couldn't get it out of his head.

He opened the door and jumped into the hall, and started climbing through the tubes toward the Drago on Ring 240. He didn't have a plan, but he didn't have time to make one, either. All he had was desperation. He prayed that it would be enough.

About halfway up, a voice echoed through the tube. "There you are." It was Spider. Zero spun around, trying to see where she was, but he couldn't find her. He kept moving, and her voice moved with him—instead of behind him, it was in front of him now, like she'd teleported. How?

"Don't stop now," said Spider. "Keep coming! Or going, if that's what you want to do. You think we can't find you? I control the ship now, you little space rat. I can find you anywhere."

Zero realized that Spider was talking through the speakers, just like Sancho had done! Which meant she'd gained even deeper access to the Pathfinder computer. That's how she knew where he was.

"The locator chip!" Zero whispered.

"What was that?" asked Spider. "You'll have to speak up, little space rat. You're so insignificant I can barely hear you." Sancho had been able to tell where Zero was by using a chip sewed into the fabric of his coverall. He unzipped it now and tore it off, leaving himself floating in the air wearing just a pair of shorts. The suit tumbled away, along with the flashlight he'd stashed inside of it. He grabbed the light, ready to use it as a club if nothing else.

"You think you can hide from me by taking off the coverall?" asked Spider. Her voice seemed to come from everywhere. "I have the whole thermal system too, dude. And you're the only other heat source on the entire ship, so: you're kind of obvious."

Zero launched himself up through the tube, leaping from Ring to Ring, trying to go as fast as he could—until *bam!* A hand reached out and grabbed him.

"Gotcha," said Spider, right in his ear.

Zero swung the flashlight at her hand, smashing her fingers. She yelped, and he jumped back down the tube. She recovered and followed him. He looked at the painted sign on the wall: Ring 193, Section B. He was almost by his family! That gave him an idea. He threw himself down the next tube, trusting that even though Spider could find him, he could at least move faster than she could.

"You can't run forever," she said through the speakers.

I'm counting on it, thought Zero, and dropped out of the tube into Ring 181. He pushed off the wall and flew down the aisle toward his family, and toward his stuff: the food, the brushes, the paint cans, and the chain. He grabbed the chain, looped it through the handle on the nearest can of paint, and started whirling it around himself like a weapon. Blue paint sprayed out at first, flying through the air in an expanding spiral, but as his swing sped up the centripetal force kept the rest of the paint firmly in the can. Spider came around the corner and he let go of the chain—it flew toward her with terrifying speed, and she grunted when it caught her squarely in the gut. He jumped off the nearest stasis pod and launched himself at her, hoping he could reach her before she recovered, but she pulled out a stun gun and fired it at him. He grabbed a stasis pod and yanked himself to the side just in time; the metal darts flew past him, sparking in the air.

"I am going to really enjoy hurting you," she said.

"With what?" asked Zero, trying to catch his breath. "You just wasted your stun gun."

Spider smiled, and pulled a second stun gun from a holster on her belt. "Surprise."

"Crap," said Zero, and reached down desperately for a weapon. All he found were the other paint cans, and he started throwing them at her wildly. A splash of color hit her face, and she howled and shielded her eyes. The narrow aisle filled with paint, covering the walls and the stasis pods and the lights, and as the lights got covered up, the aisle grew darker. Zero saw the darkness, made a quick decision, and started targeting the lights specifically. Soon the entire aisle was plunged into black.

"You think you can hide from me?" she asked.

Zero hid in the dark. "You know I'm in this aisle," said Zero, clutching his flashlight, "but do you know where? You can't aim a stun gun at computer data."

"It's always the same with you cavemen," said Spider. "You've got paper and rocks and scissors, and you think you rule the world. But advanced technology will beat you every time." Her face lit up suddenly, and he saw green lights on a pair of goggles. Her night vision! She'd used them before, trying to find him in the computer banks! They worked by amplifying light, taking the tiny amount that was present in the aisle and magnifying it so that she could see perfectly.

She aimed the stun gun straight at him and smiled. "Say hi to the other cavemen for me."

"Wrong caveman," said Zero, and held up his flashlight. "This one invented fire." He turned on the light and aimed the bright LED beam straight into her eyes; the goggles magnified the brightness and blinded her. She screamed and ripped the goggles off, trying to save her eyes, and Zero grabbed the last can left in the aisle and threw it at her—but it wasn't a paint can this time. It was the jar of jalapeños. The spicy pepper juice flew out in a cloud and hit her square in the face, right in her wide-open eyes, and the acids went to work on her eyeballs. She screamed, clawing at her face.

"What have you done?"

Zero jumped forward, staying below her flailing arms, and plucked her communicator off her belt. She swung at him—missing completely—and Zero jumped away again.

"Sorry about your eyes," he said. "I recommend you get back to the Drago, and fast."

"I'll kill you!" she screamed.

"Yeah, people keep saying that," said Zero, and launched himself up another maintenance tube.

He angled toward the fore of the ship. It was time to end this, once and for all.

CHAPTER 25

LIFE SUPPORT

As Zero jumped from Ring to Ring, he realized that he was leaving paint prints everywhere he went—not just little smears like before, but giant blobs and handprints. He looked down at himself and saw that he was covered in paint from head to toe: green and yellow and orange and black, most of it covered with a thick layer of blue. There was nothing he could do about it now, though, so he kept jumping. He had to find the other pirates while he still had the element of surprise.

The communicator he'd stolen from Spider crackled in his hand—out loud this time, because he didn't have the headphones anymore. It was Mama's voice:

"Spider?" said Mama. "Spider, did you find him?" Zero didn't answer, and a few moments later it crackled again. "Spider, where are you? Why aren't you answering?"

"Maybe he got her," said Jim.

"He's a little boy, Jim, how's he going to 'get' anybody? If I hear one more—oh no. Here it goes again." Zero heard a long, loud, farting noise, so disgusting it almost made him gag. "I've never been this sick before in my life," said Mama.

Zero couldn't help but wonder about Nyx—where was she? What was she doing? And why hadn't she told her family where he was?

Was she trying to protect him?

Zero raced all the way to the fore, then hovered out of sight near the entrance to the rec room, trying to psych himself up. This is where his lack of a plan became a serious problem. Should he just jump into the room and start yelling? Would they even take him seriously? He was a scrawny, half-naked weirdo covered with paint. What would he do if they just laughed?

He listened, knowing that Mama had to be close by, but he couldn't hear anything. This was the only place with a restroom—she had to be here. He peeked around the corner, and his hand left messy blue paint smears on the bulkhead. He tried to wipe the smear away, but all he did was make a bigger mess.

"I found her," said Jim. "Spider's on Ring 206, totally unconscious. She's covered with some kind of colorful slime, and her eyes are all red and puffy. Looks like she was blinded —probably some kind of acid."

Mama sounded furious: "If you tell me it's aliens—"

"What else is it going to be?"

Zero frowned. He'd left Spider on Ring 181—had she gotten to 206 by herself, totally blind? How? And why was she unconscious?

Whatever the answer was, both Mama and Jim had been shouting into their communicators, and Zero hadn't heard a peep out of the rec room. He didn't think anyone was in it.

A moment later, Mama confirmed his suspicions: "Just bring her to me in the Drago. We've got that first aid kit. Do you know if she was able to finish the flight plan?"

"Totally finished," said Jim. "And automated. As soon as we clear the Kuiper Belt, the new route will engage automatically, and we'll go straight to Tacita."

"Good," said Mama. "Now get her in here."

Zero shook his head—that wasn't good at all. Even if he got the pirates off the ship, the Pathfinder was programmed to betray the colonists all by itself! Everything he'd worked for, everything he'd accomplished, would be completely undone. Zero jumped past the rec room to the pilot's office, desperate to try to do something, but he had no idea what to do. He wasn't a pilot or a programmer or anything else. In this whole mess, this was the worst thing to happen yet.

And then it got worse.

The screen on the pilot's desk was flashing a warning in large red letters: Asteroid Collision Warning.

"You have got to be kidding," shouted Zero.

And then, somehow, it got even worse than that:

"Hurry back to the Drago," said Mama on the communicator. "I've got an idea."

Zero was already halfway to the pilot's chair, desperate to stop the asteroid, but something about Mama's voice scared him even more than the alarm. He grabbed the back of the chair and listened.

"I'm on Ring 222," said Jim. "I'll be there in a second."

"I'm looking at this airlock," said Mama, "between our ship and the Pathfinder. We have full environmental controls, you realize that?"

"Thanks to my docking codes," said Jim. "I gave us full access."

"And we're going to use them," said Mama. "When you get back, we can seal our doors and then vent the Pathfinder's oxygen into space. That'll get this brat."

"No," said Zero. "No, no, no, no." He looked at the communicator in his hand, and almost hit the button and repeated the outburst directly to Mama. Venting the oxygen would kill him—there'd be no way to save himself.

He tapped the asteroid warning, pulling up the full report: it was more than an hour away. It would kill him, yes, but venting the atmosphere would kill him faster. He had to solve that problem first.

Another voice crackled through the communicator: "You can't do that!" It was Nyx, and by the sound of it she was as shocked as he was. Wasn't she on the Drago? She shouted again: "What about me?"

"What about you, you little traitor?" asked Mama. "I do everything for you. I give everything to you. And then you find the kid that's doing all this, and you let him go! You refuse to tell us where he is!"

"Because I didn't want you to kill him!" cried Nyx.

Zero reeled: Nyx *was* helping him. And now her family was going to kill her for it.

"This is going to make us rich," said Mama. "We're not stealing a ship; we're creating a planet—a whole civilization! Thousands of years from now, people are going to look back on the glorious empire of Tacita, and they're not going to care about one obnoxious little brat who tried to stop it all from happening."

"I refuse to be one of the bad guys," said Nyx.

"Your loss," snarled Mama. "Let's see how long you can hold your breath."

CHAPTER 26

THE ALIEN

ZERO JUMPED OUT THE DOOR AND RACED BACK DOWN THE central column, heedless now of being seen. If he didn't make it to the Drago before Jim and Spider did, he was dead anyway. Every time he landed from a jump he felt like he was gluing himself to the new surface, thanks to all the paint, and had to peel himself off again on the next leap. He jumped from wall to wall and strut to strut, racing sixty Rings down until he arrived at 240, and then charging into the cross-hall toward the docked Drago. He saw Jim pulling Spider's floating, unconscious body through the docking Ring, and cursed himself for being too late. But Mama wasn't standing by the control panel, yet. So he still had time.

"We're here!" shouted Jim. "Where are you?"

"In the bathroom!" she shouted back. "Where do you think!"

Jim pushed Spider toward the wall of the Drago's main-room, looped one of her arms through a cargo net, and floated to the bathroom door. That meant all of the pirates were aboard the Drago. Zero looked at the airlock door.

There were two control panels that ran it—one inside the Drago, and one inside the Pathfinder. If they closed the doors, Zero could leap out and disconnect the docking clamps—cutting their connection to the Pathfinder's system before they had a chance to ruin the atmosphere. But only if they actually closed the door. He ducked around a corner, waiting for his chance.

"Do it now," shouted Mama from the bathroom. "Seal the doors, and vent the oxygen in the Pathfinder!"

"Nyx is still out there!"

"Nyx betrayed us," said Mama. "She had a chance to catch that boy and she gave it away—she's nothing but trouble, just like her no-good mother."

"She's your granddaughter—"

"Not with that attitude, she isn't," said Mama. Then her voice changed, no longer angry but subtle and cajoling. "Besides, she isn't even the real threat, is she?"

"You mean the boy?"

"I mean the alien."

Jim froze, and Zero as well. Was she just trying to convince Jim, or was the alien real? Was that how Spider ended up unconscious?

Zero glanced around himself, suddenly mistrusting everything he'd seen and heard on the Pathfinder. Was there really an alien? He hadn't believed Jim before—nobody had —but what if it was true? Out here, in the farthest reaches of the solar system, in the dark and the cold and the vast, endless mystery. Who's to say what was real and what wasn't?

"An alien?" said Jim. "You really think it might be out there?"

"Obviously there are aliens *out there*," said Mama. "I'm more worried about the aliens *in here with us*."

Zero peeked around the corner again, just the barest glimpse, showing as little of himself as he could. He ducked back out of sight again instantly. Jim was standing in the middle of the Drago's docking Ring, his wide eyes darting around as he scanned the Pathfinder for any sign of movement or sound or creepy alien invaders. Had he seen Zero? Surely he would have shouted or screamed. Especially with Zero painted bright blue, smeared with orange dots and green stripes and—

A beautiful, glorious, wonderful idea struck Zero like a thunderbolt, and he almost laughed out loud.

"Hey, Nyx?" said Jim. Zero scrambled to turn down the volume on his communicator, hoping that if Jim heard it, he'd pass it off as an echo. "I, uh, I really need to close this door right now. For the safety of ... everybody. If you haven't been ... eaten, or whatever, uh, please come back as soon as you can. Okay."

"Oh, for crying out loud!" shouted Mama. "Just close the door!"

Zero held the communicator close to his mouth, pushed the button, and made a soft gargling noise.

"What was that?" shouted Jim. "Did you hear that? There was something on the communicator. Nyx! Nyx, is that you?"

Zero did it again, and then let go of the communicator, letting it float in the narrow aisle. He cupped his hands around his mouth, trying to amplify the sound, and made the noise again: a low, soft gurgle, like an alien purr. He moved his lips while he did it, changing the tone and the pitch: "G-g-g-g-g-g-g-g-g-g-g-g-g."

"Is anybody else hearing that?" asked Jim.

"It's just Nyx screwing around," said Mama.

"That's not me," said Nyx. Zero made the noise again, louder and more angry, talking over the top of her to make sure Jim knew she was telling the truth. He floated farther back in the aisle, found a gap near the base of a stasis pod, and wedged his flashlight underneath it, pointing it toward the wide cross-hall where Jim was standing. He took a deep breath, psyching himself up, and turned it on. A large, bright circle appeared on the wall, right where Jim would have a perfect view of it.

"Aahhh!" Jim shouted. "What's that?"

Zero curled himself up into a ball, trying to present the most inhuman silhouette he could make, and then floated in front of the light. His shadow appeared on the wall like a jointed blob, bits of paint flaking off and drifting around him like a cloud. He moved his arms and legs slightly, watched the silhouette ripple, and made the gargling sound again.

"Marge, get out here!" Jim shouted. "Spider, wake up! I was right! Everyone come look at this thing! I was—oh no."

Zero was moving forward now, dragging himself along the wall, moving his shoulders and legs to keep his shadow constantly changing shape: a blob that twisted and undulated, with now and then a limb reaching out like a pseudopod or a tentacle.

Jim was practically screaming now: "It's getting closer! It's coming toward us! Everyone get in the Drago, I'm closing the door!"

"I'm not there yet!" shouted Nyx over the communicator.

"Too late," said Jim. "I'm not getting my brain sucked out by an alien monster. Closing the doors now—aahhhh!"

Zero reached the end of the aisle, unfolded into a humanoid shape, and launched himself around the corner, straight at Jim, gurgling and screaming and hissing. Zero twisted his face into a snarl, showing his teeth, and hoped his bright blue skin would do the trick. Jim shrieked in terror, eyes as wide as cereal bowls, watching Zero's approach with abject fright and moving desperately backward into the Drago. He moved toward the airlock control panel, and then past it—Zero's plan had worked too well! Jim was so scared, he couldn't even reach the controls to close the door.

Zero had to close the airlock himself. He caught the edge of the open door, pulling himself to the side, then let out a shriek of his own when a massive shape loomed up at the edge of his vision. A man in a space suit, emerging from another aisle. The man took off his helmet.

It was Kratt.

"Hello, kid," said Kratt, looking at Zero with predatory hatred. "It's time for some payback."

CHAPTER 27

PAYBACK

ZERO STARED AT KRATT IN SHOCK. "BUT ... YOU WERE outside! You were chained to a hook on the hull of the Drago!"

Kratt grinned, and held up the long length of chain still welded to the back of his suit. The other end was welded to a piece of the Drago's hull, now floating torn and bent on the edge of the chain. "I ripped it off," said Kratt. "It's amazing what you can you do with all that free time and nowhere to go."

Zero searched for a response, too scared to think, but before he could form any words, Kratt swung the chain sharply through the air, using the broken chunk of hull like a medieval morning star. Zero pushed himself backward to get away, and the piece of hull whistled past his ear, missing him by centimeters. Kratt snapped the chain around and whipped it out again, never giving Zero a nanosecond to gather himself. Zero had to keep moving backward, tumbling and scrambling, just to keep from getting his head crushed.

"Look out, Kratt!" yelled Jim. "It's an alien!"

"Shut up!" Kratt yelled back, and pressed forward still attacking. He slammed the hull fragment back and forth through the hallway, throwing off sparks as it clanged from one bulkhead to another. "Ten hours!" screamed Kratt. "You locked me outside for ten hours! No food, no sound; no one coming to help me or save me or even talk to me!"

"Kratt!" said Mama, emerging from the bathroom with a weary expression. "You're back."

"You shut up, too!" screamed Kratt. "He locked me out there, but you left me out there!"

"Don't you talk to me that way—"

"I'll talk to you any way I like!" yelled Kratt. He turned back toward the Drago, and pointed at Mama with fire in his eyes. "I'm coming for you next."

Kratt was only turned around for a second, but that gave Zero the time he needed to back up farther, regain his bearings, and come up with a plan. It wasn't much of a plan— jump into the central column and get away—but it was all Zero had time for. He curled up his legs, getting ready to kick off the wall and leap across the open space, but the paint on his feet had dried now. It wasn't slimy, and it wasn't tacky, it was just hard and slick; when his foot hit the wall to jump away, he slipped, giving him just a bare minimum of momentum. He tumbled into the center of the column slowly, almost painfully slowly, turning slightly in the air. He remembered what Sancho had said about the ship: *there's no gravity, but there's still air, and that means there's air resistance. If you run out of momentum, you'll stop, and if you don't have anything to push off of, you'll be stuck.*

"No no no no no!" said Zero, stretching frantically for

anything he could reach, but it was no good. He slowed to a stop.

Right in the center of the wide central column.

"Well, well, well," said Kratt, floating at the entrance to the cross-hall. "Who's stuck now?"

"I was only trying to defend my ship," said Zero. "That's all. You would have done the same thing."

"No, I wouldn't have," said Kratt, and whipped his make-shift chain weapon into the side of the bulkhead. The loud *CLANG* reverberated through the whole ship. "I would have killed you." He drifted slightly closer. "No fuss, no muss, no shocking last-minute reappearance." He dragged his thumb across his throat as he drifted slightly closer. "Just khhhhht! Dead."

"But I didn't hurt you," said Zero.

"What?"

"I mean I didn't physically harm you! I didn't throw you into space or cut a hole in your suit or anything like that—I could have, but I didn't. That's got to be worth something, right?"

"I'll tell you what that's worth," said Kratt. "You tell me your name, and when I cook you and eat you I'll name whatever dish I make after you. The ... Frankie Feast. The Little Danny Dumpling." Zero didn't speak—his brain was too frightened to come up with words or sentences. Kratt roared and swung his chain. "What's your name?"

"Zero!" said Zero. "My name is Zero."

"That's a very appropriate name for you," said Kratt. He drifted even closer now—well within reach of the long, terrifying chain. "Because you're a worthless, pointless, useless little lump. Killing you will bring me more joy than you've ever brought to anyone in your life."

Zero shrank back, trying to swim through the air, but he didn't move an inch. He winced, expecting a blow from the chain at any moment, but over Kratt's shoulder he saw Jim and Mama huddled around their control panel, whispering and arguing and—every couple of seconds—looking over their shoulders at him.

No, not at him. At Kratt.

"They're going to lock you out," said Zero.

Kratt flashed an evil smile, indulging his prey before he pounced and killed it. "Out of what?"

"Out of the Drago," said Zero. "They're going to vent the atmosphere, didn't you hear? They're going to seal their door shut and then open a bunch of airlocks. The Pathfinder will just be a giant empty can—no oxygen, no nothing."

"You're lying."

"Look at them!" said Zero. "They're doing it right now!"

Kratt studied Zero carefully, making sure this wasn't some kind of a trick to let Zero escape when his back was turned, and then glanced over his shoulder. When he saw them working on the console, he grabbed the edge of bulkhead, turned himself around, and shouted:

"You wouldn't dare!"

Mama looked up at him, her face a mixture of fear and fury, and then looked back down at the console.

"They already said they'll leave Nyx," said Zero.

"I heard them," Kratt growled.

"And you just threatened to kill them," said Zero. "You think they won't leave you, too?"

"Stop it," said Kratt. Jim and Mama kept working, and he

yelled louder. "Stop it!" He shook his head, and thought for a moment, then looked back at Zero and laughed. "They're not going to hurt me, you idiot! They know I'm safe because I'm wearing a spacesu ..." He trailed off, looking around. "Where's my helmet?"

"You took it off," said Zero. "Back by the door, remember? It's okay, though—it looks like Jim picked it up." Zero pointed, and Kratt turned back to look, and Jim quickly hid the large helmet behind his back, looking guilty.

"Raaahhhhh!" Kratt roared and launched himself at the docking Ring. Mama finished typing something and slammed her hand down on a button.

The airlock doors began to close.

CHAPTER 28

THE LAST MINUTE

KRATT WHIPPED OUT HIS CHAIN AS HE FLEW, WHIPPING THE chunk of broken hull forward and lodging it right between the doors as they tried to slide together. The doors stalled, and Kratt slammed into them like a human missile.

"Get away!" shouted Mama. She poked at him with a pole from the wall, shoving it through the gap in the doors, trying to push Kratt away. "Jim, get him away from the door!"

"I'm trying," said Jim, "I'm trying!" He didn't have a pole, so he was pushing with his hands and feet. Kratt was pushing back, scrabbling at the door like a wild animal; he didn't say anything at all, just shouted in incoherent rage.

"This keeps getting worse," Zero muttered. If they damaged the door, Zero might not ever be able to close it again—and that asteroid was still coming toward them. There were at least three different calamities trying to end his life right now, and he couldn't do anything about any of them. He tried again to move from the center of the empty column, but he couldn't go anywhere.

"Krattison Oswald Hendricksiter!" yelled Mama. "You get away from this door this instant!"

"Not this time!" roared Kratt, and slammed his fist against the half-closed door. "No more calling me an idiot!" He slammed his fist again. "No more 'sorry, Mama!'" Jim tried to punch him, but Kratt grabbed his arm and pulled him forward, bonking Jim's head into the inside of the door.

"You're going to break the ship!" Zero yelled.

"It's my ship now," yelled Kratt, and wrenched the pole out of Mama's hands. "I'm the new leader of this pirate crew, and I can do anything I want!"

"You're not even on the crew anymore!" said Mama. She grabbed one of his arms, and Jim grabbed another, and Kratt fought back like a caged wolf.

"I've decided you're right," said Nyx. Zero spun around and saw her floating close behind him. "I'd rather ditch these losers and come with you to the colony."

"Nyx!" Zero tried to shout and whisper at the same time. "Quick, shove me over there!"

"I'll do better than that," said Nyx, and held up a stun gun. "Turns out Spider had three of these."

Zero's eyes went wide. "You're the one who knocked her out?"

"Of course it was me," said Nyx. "Who'd you think it was, an alien?" She shoved him hard, sending herself toward the Drago and Zero away from it. He twisted in the air, hit the wall with his feet, and jumped as hard as he could to follow her. Still in midair, Nyx raised her stun gun, aimed it at the tangle of bodies, and fired. The little metal darts shot out, went right past Kratt, and hit Mama square in the shoulder. She froze in place, shaking slightly, and the current passed through her into Kratt, and through him into Jim, and all three of them were shocked and vibrating. The three pirates fell to the floor, and Nyx and Zero landed next to them. They shoved them through the gap and into the Drago.

"Ow," said Kratt, apparently just conscious enough to speak in a low, slurred voice, but not conscious enough to resist. Zero and Nyx were able to maneuver his floating body through the gap and into the cluttered pirate ship.

Zero tried to dislodge the piece of hull plating Kratt had jammed into the door, but it wouldn't budge. The door was still trying to close, and the metal chunk was holding it open, and Zero couldn't move either one.

"Stand back," said Nyx, and hit a button on the nearby console, and the door started to open instead of close. The chunk of metal drifted free.

"Smart," said Zero.

"Thanks," said Nyx.

Zero kicked the metal and the floating chain through the door, and Nyx hit the button to close it again. A small screen showed an image of the other side of the door, and he watched as the Drago's airlock closed tight, sealing the pirates inside. A green sign lit up, showing two words: Airlock Secure.

"Golden," said Zero.

"I'm glad it sealed their side," said Nyx. "I didn't want to kill them, you know?"

"Yeah," said Zero. "They're awful, but me neither." He pushed the button to disengage the docking clamps, and watched through the camera as the Drago drifted away from the Pathfinder.

"Okay," said Nyx. "If I'm counting right, we have half an

hour to reboot Sancho before my mom's new flight plan takes us to Tacita."

Zero looked at her in surprise. "How do you know about rebooting Sancho?"

"I wanted to see what you'd been doing in that empty hangar, so I found a space suit and went out to look. I found your little viewscreen with the reboot instructions," said Nyx. "Pretty clever to hide it out there."

"Have I kept *any* secrets from you so far?"

"Not really."

"But you never sold me out to your family."

"They're not much of a family," said Nyx. "It still took me a while to choose a side, though. Sorry I waited so long."

"As far as I'm concerned, you're the hero of the day," said Zero. "Can you reboot Sancho?"

"I think so. What are you going to do?"

"If I'm counting correctly," said Zero, "I have a little less than half an hour to get back upstairs and shoot an asteroid out of our way." He tried to smile, but it only looked pained and sour. "Or everyone on this ship is going to die."

CHAPTER 29
BEDTIME

ZERO AND NYX PUSHED THEMSELVES INTO THE CENTRAL column, and then jumped toward the fore of the ship as hard as they could. They were relatively close, so it only took a couple of jumps; Zero had spent so long crawling through the maintenance tubes, he'd forgotten how fast it was to move through the center. He didn't have time to enjoy it, though: he had to move as fast as he could.

"Do you know how to shoot down an asteroid?" asked Nyx.

"I did it once before," said Zero. "I think I can probably do it again."

"You *think* you can *probably* do it again?"

"I had Sancho's help the last time," said Zero, feeling defensive. "Can you get him turned on?"

"Say what you will about my awful family," said Nyx, grabbing a metal strut and kicking off it, launching herself toward the next one. "Spider was a technical genius, and I learned everything I could from her. I'm pretty sure I can reboot a computer." She caught the last strut and aimed herself at the door to the computer room. "Good luck."

"Good luck," said Zero. He held out his hand, and she grabbed it firmly, staring at him.

"Nice body paint, by the way," said Nyx. "You're going to start a trend."

"Thanks," said Zero. "And—I'm glad you're here. I'm glad I'm not alone."

Nyx grinned. "Me too."

They let go and jumped toward their final destinations. She disappeared into the dark door of the computer room, and he sailed into the pilot's office. The viewscreen on the desk was going crazy now, with red lights flashing and sirens blaring and bright, glowing words lighting up the walls: Asteroid Collision Imminent! Emergency Action Required!

"I'm here!" Zero said, grabbing the pilot's chair and strapping himself in.

"Asteroid collision imminent," said a voice.

"Sancho, is that you?"

"Asteroid collision imminent."

Just a recorded warning, then, thought Zero. *I think I can remember how this works.*

He stared at the desk, trying to remember the procedure. He started by tapping every viewscreen he could reach, trying to wake them up; most of them turned into holographic displays of the ship and the Kuiper Belt, but some just kept flashing their alarm signs. The biggest display was on the desk itself, which lit up with a large, detailed hologram. Zero saw the Pathfinder, and a line showing its course, and a bright pink X marked "Engage New Flight Plan." The line beyond the X curved, veering sharply to the left—or as sharply as anything can veer when it's traveling at four million kilometers per hour.

"So that's where Spider's program kicks in to take us to Tacita," said Zero. A small holographic readout next to the X showed their estimated time of arrival: fourteen minutes and fifty-two seconds. Fifty-one seconds. Fifty. Forty-nine. Zero tore his eyes away from the countdown to look at the other display, even more terrifying than the first: a thin, purple line labeled "Asteroid 54987," intercepting their path on a perfect collision course. The intercept point was marked with a purple X, just in front of the pink X, and the countdown was sooner: six minutes and twenty-seven seconds. Twenty-six. Twenty-five.

"Come on, Zero, focus." He shook his head, trying to remember how the force cannons worked. He had to touch the display, right? He reached out and tapped the hologram of the asteroid—and the ship responded with another automated warning:

"Do you wish to calculate a new route to the designated destination?"

"What?" asked Zero. "No, no! Don't fly to the asteroid, you dumb spaceship. Shoot it!" He canceled the request. He had to do something else—not just tap it, but ... slap it? He tried slapping it, swatting his hand through the hologram like he was swatting a fly. Nothing. He tried to push it back. He tried to pull it to the side. He tried flicking it away like a crumb on a napkin, but nothing worked. Finally, he simply reached out and grabbed the hologram, too frustrated to come up with anything better, and the desk responded again:

"Do you wish to fire force cannons at the designated target?"

"Yes! Shoot it!" said Zero. But it wasn't voice activated. He had to tap something to make it work, but he couldn't remember what or how. He let go, thinking that might do it, but all the message did was disappear.

"Asteroid Collision Imminent," said the warning, and the timer continued counting down: three minutes and two seconds. Three minutes and one second. Three minutes. Two minutes and fifty-nine seconds.

Zero grabbed the holographic asteroid again, and the message reappeared: Did he want to fire the force cannons? Sancho had told him the ship couldn't fire on its own; a human had to give the order. How had he done it last time? He'd moved it or twisted it or—

"Twist!" shouted Zero, and twisted his hand to the right.

"Target confirmed," said the message on the desk. "Firing force cannons." Zero waited, watching as a new line flew out from the front of the Pathfinder, slicing through space toward the asteroid. It hit, and the asteroid changed course, and Zero screamed in triumph.

"Yes!"

The desktop screen lit up with a friendly, yellow circle. "Hello," said the computer voice. "I am the Pathfinder's navigational artificial intelligence. You may call me Sancho."

"Sancho!" screamed Zero, still too excited from his victory to quiet down. "Are you back?"

"I think so," said Nyx, floating into the room behind him. "I followed the procedure exactly, and all the right lights lit up." She looked at the hologram display. "I heard you shout 'yes' super loud, so I assume you stopped the asteroid?"

"Got it," said Zero. "Hey Sancho, can you hear me?"

"I can detect two voices through the microphones in the pilot's office," said Sancho. "Neither of you are wearing locator chips, so I must assume that you are not supposed to be here. Are you the pirates who attacked this vessel?"

"Sort of," said Nyx.

"It's me, Sancho," said Zero, "it's Zero! Don't you remember?"

"I am a navigational computer," said Sancho. "I do not have the capacity to differentiate one human voice from another. Are you Mr. Huang?"

Nyx frowned. "Is he always like this?"

"Always," said Zero. "Sancho, yes, I'm Su-Shu Huang. It's good to have you back. The pirates are gone, except for one, but she's good and she's coming with us. When they turned you off they programmed a new route into the guidance computer, trying to take us to a secret planet called Tacita. The Pathfinder is automated to change course as soon as we cross the Kuiper Cliff, in ..." He looked at the timer display. "Ten minutes. Can you turn that off and put us back on the original route?"

"I will attempt to do so," said Sancho.

Zero looked at Nyx. "This might take him a while—"

"I have successfully returned us to the original route," said Sancho.

"Not bad," said Nyx. "Kind of crappy at voice recognition but, let's be fair, honestly a super-good navigational computer."

"Thank you," said Sancho. "Now: may I ask which one of you is going to use the pilot's stasis pod?"

And then Zero remembered, and the whole world

seemed to stand still. "There's only one," he said. He looked at Nyx, his eyes wide in shock. "There's only one stasis pod."

Nyx stared back, realization dawning on her face. "Wh —what?"

The desktop viewscreen changed again, this time showing an old-timey phone icon, and two bright blue words: Incoming Message.

Zero frowned. "Who could be calling us?"

"Who do you think?" asked Nyx, and leaned forward to tap the screen. The words disappeared, replaced by the faces of Mama, Jim, Kratt, and Spider, all clustered around a screen of their own in the cockpit of the Drago.

Mama smiled with a frightening blend of sweetness and spite. "Hello, children."

Nyx narrowed her eyes. "What do you want?"

"Your heads on a stick," growled Kratt.

"Quiet, you," snapped Mama, and then her sickly smile returned. "We want our ship back."

"It's not your ship," said Zero.

"It was," said Mama, "and in a couple of minutes, it will be again. What we're giving you now is the opportunity to get back in our good graces. When we get back on board that ship—and we will—you want to be our friends, right? Not our enemies."

Sancho spoke up: "The reboot process appears to have deleted the virus in my software that prevented me from detecting their ship. I can see it clearly on my sensors, attempting to redock at a different airlock."

"Don't let it," said Nyx.

"I will not," said Sancho.

"There's no code you can use that I can't break," said

Spider.

"Look," said Zero. "You can't come on board, and you can't have the ship. In about eight minutes we're going to Boost the Medina drive, and head off to Kaguya at a speed that will literally kill you if you're not in a stasis pod." He pointed over his shoulder. "Nyx is taking this one, and I'm going to keep you away from her and from everybody on this ship until my last breath."

"But Nyx is on our side!" cried Mama. "You fool! This was all part of our plan: you feel sorry for her, take her into your confidence, and now when you least expect, she *strikes!*" The pirates froze, waiting. After a moment, Mama said it again. "She *strikes!*"

Zero looked at Nyx. "You're not going to strike, right?"

Nyx sneered. "Pshh. Of course not." She looked at the pirates on the screen. "Are you seriously trying to bluff me with a plan that I clearly know is not real?"

"We're giving you a chance to come back to your family," said Jim.

"You're not my family," said Nyx. "You're just the criminals I couldn't get away from until now. And now I'm getting away to a place where you'll never be able to follow me."

"You're giving us up for a nobody," said Kratt. "He's nothing. Even his name is Zero!"

Zero rose out of his chair. "My name is Su-Shu Huang. And this is my ship, and Nyx is my friend, and you can't have any of them." The pirates started to protest, but he reached out and tapped the screen, closing the call. "So stay out."

"Su-Shu, huh?" asked Nyx.

Zero shrugged. "Yeah, it's kind of a dumb name."

"I think it's cool," said Nyx. "My name is, um ..." She

trailed off, like she was embarrassed of it. "Catherine."

Zero raised his eyebrow. "You really don't look like a Catherine."

Nyx smiled. "Tell me about it."

"I have scrambled the airlocks in such a way that it will take them at least ten minutes to hack through. We are scheduled to Boost the Medina StarDrive in six minutes," said Sancho. "The stasis pod initiation process takes four. Whichever one of you is going to use the pod needs to get into it immediately."

"You," said Zero.

"And leave you to die?" asked Nyx. "No way."

"But we have to—"

"We can share it," said Nyx, and pulled him over to it. It was designed for an adult, just like the pod Zero had been in before, which meant there was more than enough room to fit two children. She hit the button on the side and the door swung open.

"Are you sure?" asked Zero.

"Stop arguing," said Nyx, and then broke into a smile. "Just try not to get your paint all over me, okay?"

"Okay," said Zero, and took her hand. They stepped in together, squeezing in next to each other, and then the pod door swung closed again.

"I'm kind of scared," said Nyx.

"Of the pod?"

"Of the future," she said. "It's a long way away."

"It's okay," said Zero, already feeling sleepy. He held her hand tightly. "It's gonna be great."

And then the gel started to fill up the pod, and then he was asleep.

CHAPTER 30

TOMORROW

ZERO WAS SWIMMING AGAIN, LIKE A DOLPHIN IN AN OCEAN THE size of the universe. He turned and dove and danced through the water, until at some point it occurred to him that he had felt like this before. When had that been? He'd been doing something, or thinking something, or ... oh yeah. ... It had been a dream. He wondered if that meant this was a dream, too.

And that's all it took to wake him up.

The stasis effect wore off more quickly this time, and the pod worked the way it was supposed to: the sticky gel that surrounded him drained out the bottom, and the door swung open with a smooth, satisfying motion. It happened so quickly, in fact, that Zero was already floating out of the pod before he noticed the tall, stern woman hovering in front of him.

"You're not the pilot we left home with," she said. She was wearing a United Earth uniform. "Neither of you are."

Zero's eyes went wide. "Uh—um—uh."

"Hi," said Nyx, floating out next to Zero. "We can explain."

"Sancho filled me in on most of it," said the woman. She looked at Zero. "Your name is Su-Shu Huang, and your pod malfunctioned, and then Jim Gaynor betrayed his post and brought a crew of pirates aboard." She looked at Nyx. "I take it you're one of the pirates."

"My *family* were the pirates," said Nyx. "I kept trying to ... tell them to ... be good? And stuff? But I'm just thirteen years old. They never listen to anything I say—"

"It's fine," said the woman. "You're not in trouble. In fact, let's make this official." She held out her hand, shaking each kid's hand in turn. "My name is Tamira Hatendi of the United Earth Fleet, Head of the Pathfinder mission and Governor of the Kaguya Colony. You've saved our ship and the lives of everyone on it. Please allow me to be the first to thank you, from the bottom of my heart. As soon as the colony is established, at our very first meeting, I will award you our highest—and at this point, only—honor."

Zero didn't know what to say. "Thank you!"

"No," said Governor Hatendi. "Thank *you*. As I understand it, without you two helping us back there, we'd been living in a mine right now."

"Even as a purely navigational computer," said Sancho, "I can see that you deserve this honor very much."

"Thanks, buddy," said Zero.

"You said we helped you 'back there,'" said Nyx. "How far back is 'back there'?"

Governor Hatendi smiled. "One hundred and five years ago," she said, and gestured to the window. "We're in orbit around Kaguya—have a look."

"What?" Zero could barely contain himself—he pushed off of the stasis pod and flew across the room to the window. A giant blue marble appeared below them, blue and green and white.

"It looks like Earth," Nyx whispered. "I mean—it looks like the pictures of Earth. I've never actually seen it."

"The continents are all different," said Zero. "And Kaguya has way more islands."

"Most of the landmass is in a single archipelago," said Hatendi. "Though there is one large continent, just out of sight around the curve to your right. It'll rotate back around again in about an hour." She pointed to the edge of the planet. "That's where we're landing three days from now."

Nyx was in awe. "It's the most beautiful thing I've ever seen."

"What do you mean 'three days'?" asked Zero. "I thought we were going to wake up right when it was time to land?"

"Most of the passengers, yes," said Sancho. "Governor Hatendi was awakened early this morning to assist with the preparations, and after I explained the situation she insisted on waking the two of you early, as well."

"What can I say?" asked Hatendi. "I couldn't wait to talk to you."

"Is my family okay?" asked Zero.

"Every passenger is safe and accounted for," said Hatendi, "including your family. Would you like to see them?"

"Maybe in a bit," said Zero. "Honestly, right now I'm just starving."

"Me too," said Nyx.

"Sounds good to me," said Hatendi. "Why don't we move

into the rec room, and we can talk more over food. There are a lot of preparations to make before we land, and a whole new world to explore, and not all of my staff is awake yet." She smiled. "I could use your help."

"Done," said Nyx with a grin.

"Let's go," said Zero, and smiled. "I'll make you my specialty: a double-sized, one-of-a-kind Zero burger, with floating fries and ketchup."

"And a side of baby carrots," added Sancho.

ACKNOWLEDGMENTS

Huge thanks to my agent, Sara Crowe, my editor, Heather Alexander, and my wife, Dawn. Also to my children, off of whom I bounced a thousand ideas, and to my brother, Robison Wells, who helped me come up with the core of the story. Last but not least, a massive thank you to all the fans who listened to Zero's story in Audible, and helped to make it such a success. We wouldn't be here without you.

ABOUT THE AUTHOR

Dan Wells writes a lot of books for teens and adults. *Zero G* is his first book for children. In addition to science fiction, he also writes horror, fantasy, thrillers, and historical fiction. Dan lives in Utah with his wife, six children, two dogs he loves, and a rabbit he tolerates.

www.thedanwells.com

 facebook.com/TheDanWells
twitter.com/TheDanWells
instagram.com/authordanwells

Made in the USA
Middletown, DE
24 March 2022

63042071R00109